The Last of Deeds

EOIN McNAMEE was born in Kilkeel, County Down, in 1961. *The Last of Deeds* was shortlisted for the 1989 *Irish Times*/Aer Lingus Award for Irish Literature. He was awarded the Macauley Fellowship for Irish Literature in 1990. He has also written a novel, *Resurrection Man*.

Also by Eoin McNamee in Picador

RESURRECTION MAN

EOIN McNAMEE

The Last of Deeds
& Love in History

PICADOR

The Last of Deeds first published with *The Lion Alone*
(a short version of *Love in History*) and *Radio 1974*
as *The Last of Deeds* by The Raven Arts Press 1989

This edition first published 1992 by Penguin Books Ltd

This edition published 1995 by Picador
an imprint of Macmillan General Books
Cavaye Place London SW10 9PG
and Basingstoke

Associated companies throughout the world

ISBN 0 330 33342 9

Copyright © Eoin McNamee 1989, 1992

1 3 5 7 9 8 6 4 2

A CIP catalogue record for this book is available from
the British Library

Phototypeset by Intype, London
Printed by Cox & Wyman Ltd, Reading, Berkshire

The Last of Deeds

One

We've all done it. Imagined our own funerals. The church is overflowing. There is unrestrained weeping. A woman dressed in black stands at the back of the crowd then steps forward to lay a wreath. The face is veiled but the hands are beautifully manicured, the nails long and red, cuticles stripped with orange stick and the skin so fine it is almost transparent, so that the tips of the fingers are drops of milky water. There is some scandalized whispering and men eye their wives wishing it to be over, earth rustling like sheets on the lid of the coffin.

At least that's how I imagine it. Other people probably have their own way. When they buried Deeds I eyed the crowd expectantly. If anyone had deserved a beautiful stranger it was Deeds.

Not that I wasn't used to being in graveyards. There was the time they dug up the old graveyard in the middle of the town to build a new roundabout. Deeds, Jammy and me used to go down there at night when the workmen had left. There were graves exposed everywhere and the lids of the coffins were as thin as old parchment. In one corner they had just dug up bones because it had been a paupers' graveyard and they buried the dead in a hinged deal coffin which could be used again and again.

The coffin was laid over the grave and the bottom opened so that the corpses of the poor tumbled into the earth with a wet slap.

Then again maybe they didn't make any noise at all because the corpses of the poor don't weigh anything. Maybe the gravediggers had to shovel earth into their faces so that they wouldn't float to the top again.

There was the ruin of a church in the graveyard as well with a Union Jack flying from the steeple because the dead must have some kind of politics. Binty said that some countries used to dig up the bones of soldiers from battle-fields and export them for fertilizer. Millions of bones in the holds of ships – the noise that must have made, Binty said.

Here they took the bones away in sand lorries and dumped them down at the Banks.

The first couple of nights we just walked around looking at the graves and then one evening Deeds jumped into one and put his foot through the coffin lid. He came out of the grave with a skull in his hand. Then he started going round all the graves and getting the skulls. Some of them were so old that they fell apart in his hands like waterlogged bread. When he had enough he lined them up on the wall and took out his catapult which he had made from an old piece of aluminium and the tube from a bicycle tyre. The skulls on the wall were grinning at him and he was grinning back as he blasted them to dust and fragments with steel ball bearings.

'The living revenge themselves upon the dead,' he said, and laughed.

You stand at the back of a funeral and wait for something to happen. You wait for the beautiful stranger because you know that in a few minutes the funeral will be over and men will come with shovels which will sound like torn silk when they bite into the earth and the earth will sound like sheets when it falls on the lid of the coffin and that will be the end.

On the outskirts of town there is an avenue lined with trees. The legend is that there is a red woman who waits up the Avenue at night and that she has long strangling hands. Then you learn that there are no ghosts but that Cupid's disco is beside the Avenue and the ground under the trees is littered with used condoms like worms after rain. And you learn that if you go up there on a Saturday night after Cupid's, the snap of buttons undone and the rattle of catches unfastened can be detected when the shifting and moistening of many bodies sounds like death.

The Avenue leads from Mill Street to the new estates of the Desmesne where you would think the houses are elegant if you saw them at night when the windows are lit and the smell of cooking is in the air. But during the day you can see the whitewash blacken and peel with salt carried in from the sea, and how the dune grass encroaches on lawns and gardens. And if you look closely late at night you see videos flicker behind the curtains like light undressing itself.

There were plenty of stories about the people who lived in those houses. The Scout called them readers' wives. You knew what he meant. They were like the women in the readers' wives section of porn mags with a block of print over their faces like the stamp of a prison censor. In the background of those photographs you see the things you would find in any of those houses. The settee from the discount warehouse, the leather-bound books on pine shelves, the TV, the video. And out in front birth-stretched breasts lolling like tongues out of rubber bras, and cunts like something you'd find on the dump. And the shops in town have racks full of porn mags so that you wonder where they all come from – all that pucker, glisten and gape. It might be your daughter or your sister. Someone's, anyhow.

The river goes through the centre of the town past the warehouse where Deeds and Jammy had the loft and then it empties into the Harbour. Every week a big Polish boat comes in over the bar to moor beside the Plant. The boat stays for a day or two and sometimes you can hear the music that Sharon heard and then it will go out past the pier, leaving half-slices of bread, bottles and pieces of wood coated with oil floating in corners of the Harbour.

If you stand on the pier wall where Deeds and Jammy painted their names you can see the concrete shelter on top of the Banks with the toilets at the back. There are still scorchmarks on the wall of the toilets where we lit fires. There is still a broken urinal flushing endlessly and the east wind carrying spray over the Harbour wall and through the empty doorframe of the shelter until your clothes acquire a saline odour, a deepwater smell.

Two

He got the name Deeds at school when Boyle, the principal, got him by the throat and thrust his chalky, bald head into his face and hissed 'your misdeeds will be the death of me'. Deeds had a round moon face with wire glasses that fitted his big head closely. He had hands the size of lunchboxes and his voice was soft like wings. When Jammy was listening to Deeds' voice you could tell that he wanted to reach out and touch it as if it was a bird. Jammy loved pigeons and he helped Deeds build the loft and look after the birds. Jammy always had six inches of snot hanging from his sleeve and a chinful of pimples on the verge of bursting. Deeds' hair was cropped close to his skull so that you could see blue scars through it, but Jammy had long greasy hair that got caught around his face. One day at school a teacher used Jammy's hair to lift him off his feet with Jammy saying pleasesir, pleasesir very softly.

When his father was alive Jammy lived with him in an old council house near the Harbour. His father came home every night from the pub using both sides of the road. Jammy would lie awake in bed listening for his footsteps but the only thing he would hear was the scratch of tiny

8

claws as rats chewed the house apart. Then one night Jammy's father fell into the Harbour on the way home. The scratch of tiny claws was the last thing he heard as crabs crossed the Harbour bottom to feed on the corpse.

They put the loft on top of the old warehouse on the river. They found the wood they needed on the banks of the river and covered it with scraps of paint, tar and creosote. There was a run made of chicken wire at the front. Inside they kept bags of meal, pliers for ringing the pigeons' legs, carrying baskets and ointments for toe rot and other diseases. And pigeons: blues, greys, fantails.

Deeds would take a pigeon in his cupped hands like water to blow its breastfeathers apart or stroke them against the grain with his forefinger.

'Look at that,' he would say, 'if an angel was going to fly like a pigeon it would have to have a chest ten feet wide to get off the ground.'

To safeguard the approach to the roof Deeds had come up with a system of ladders which would come away from the wall, holes in the roof disguised by loose tiles, gutters weakened so that if you put a foot wrong they would tilt and throw you into the river seventy or eighty feet below. Snakes and Ladders he called it.

He liked to sit with his legs over the edge of the roof watching pigeons fly up the river and the way they stayed close to the walls of the house on either side for protection. Sometimes Jammy would put them in baskets and they would take them out to a grey plantation of fir trees on the edge of town. Deeds would release the pigeons and watch them fly in a tight homing circle while Jammy hopped from foot to foot in case something happened to them.

It's hard to tell when things start. That's what Deeds used to say. Like one day you look up and see the settee and the pine shelves and the video and you want to know where it started and how far back you have to go. Maybe the first time you touched her and her inhalations became brief and quick. Or maybe you have to go further back than that.

We were down at the Harbour one day when Deeds said it about going to Cupid's. It was the beginning of December when the streetlights come on in the estates before it is properly dark and the smoke of fires collects closer to the roofs. Women hurry when they are carrying the shopping to their cars. The rain comes in from the sea and the sea is grey. The Orangemen stop marching through the town so that you don't hear the sound of their preachers talking through public address systems which has sounded like a radio in another room all summer.

Deeds had found a tin of paint behind the Plant. We took it up to the pier and Deeds painted his name on the pier wall. He took his time, using big letters you could see all over the Harbour. When he finished Jammy had to have his name done as well.

Jammy was pleased with it. He started to kick the empty paint tin along the pier. There were threads of paint coming out of it and wrapping themselves around his shins.

'You're not half-wise, Jammy,' Deeds said. Jammy dribbled the tin to the edge of the dock and kicked it out over the water.

'Goal,' he shouted, 'one-nil.'

The tin filled up and sank. Deeds lit a cigarette and leaned against the pier wall.

'We're going to Cupid's tomorrow night,' he said.

'What for?' Jammy asked.

'I'm going to get my hole.'

'Who with?'

'Never you mind, you chicken or something?'

Jammy tried to say something but couldn't. When he got nervous he had a speech defect where his tongue came to the edge of his lips and stayed there like some fat, shiny parasite. In the end he just shook his head.

'Anne-Marie Hicks,' Deeds said. We saw her every day in the Submarine Café.

The Submarine had yellow lace curtains hard as wax because of the grease in the air. The tables had blue plastic on top. There was a pool table in the back and a poker machine. The stainless steel urn steamed, fogging the windows. Greasespots separated and merged on the surface of the tea and you could make a tea last for the afternoon while the fish fryer crackled and drenched the air around you.

During the day she was a waitress at the Submarine. At night she was in Cupid's. If she wasn't there she was hanging round the Harbour and sometimes one of the workers from the Plant would take her behind the coastguard station and return with his heart frozen and his clothes impregnated with the smell of chip fat and salt cunt.

She had a small mouth and huge breasts, the blue and white checked nylon of her apron rustling as she walked among the tables. Deeds swore that if you listened you could hear the sound of sex as well like the dull lapping of animals drinking.

We left the Submarine and went to the loft. When we got there we sat on the edge of the roof. You could see all of Mill Street and right down the Harbour road as far as the Harbour. The streets were wet and you could see the wet blackness of the rooftiles on buildings. There were hardly any people about. Deeds took a Frenchie out of his pocket and split the foil with his thumb. He unrolled it and blew it up like a balloon. Then he tied a knot in the end and let it go. He did the same with another. We sat on the roof and watched them go down over the river like pink silk parachutes, weaving when the wind brushed them.

Three

Binty said that the Harbour used to be a big fishing port until the war, when a U-boat surfaced in the middle of the fleet. It was black with rust on the hatches, he said, as if he had been there. It had a big gun at the front, and when it submerged, fuming with compressed air escaping from valves, there were just jellyfish of oil and splintered planks where the fishing boats used to be.

Binty told Jammy that the U-boat was still out there. Half a century of polishing torpedoes and replacing detonators in cramped and fetid quarters. Surfacing at night for air or from habit. You hear stories of Japanese soldiers who have survived in the jungle for decades after the war, a picture of the emperor in their foxholes, while mildew claimed their uniforms and the bark of flying foxes claimed their minds. Jammy didn't know what to believe.

Binty lived with Minnie Toal in the shelter at the top of the Banks. The Banks were brick-coloured cliffs overlooking the shingle beach beside the Harbour. The shelter was just a concrete shed with benches in it and broken toilets at the back. Binty said it was put there so that people coming out for walks could sit in it. But nobody ever came for a walk on the Banks and there were grass clippings, old bottles and builders' rubble piled at the foot of the cliffs.

We did our drinking at the Banks. Most of the time we drank vodka. You put the bottle to your mouth, tilted it back and bolted vodka. At first it would be cold, like shutting your teeth on bone or china, but it would be warm and bitter after that, sitting outside the shelter with a fire or perched up on the roof feeling like you could reach up and touch the big, glass lip of the moon above you.

There was a car park on the Esplanade behind the Banks and cars with couples in them would park there at night. The cars would start creaking and moving after a while. Sometimes there would be fifteen or twenty cars in different parts of the car park, all moving with hollow noises. Deeds would say that the town was breeding and go over to bang on the window of a car or rip the boot into the side of it and the movement would stop. They might drive off after that, but usually the movement would start again, slowly at first.

The next night we met at the Banks about eight o'clock. Jammy went to the off-licence and Deeds lit a fire against the wall of the toilets. By the time Jammy came back the fire had caught and the sandy area around the toilets began to look like some kind of desert with Deeds sitting in the middle of it saying that he was the sheikh, the sheikh of Araby, and laughing to himself.

'Hold the bus,' Jammy said after a while, 'Minnie's on the warpath.'

I looked around and saw her coming out of the shelter. She had red eyes and grey hair with pink bald patches in it. She had a big nose like a vegetable covered in broken veins and blackheads. When she walked her bony pelvis stuck out from under her skirt. But it was her stomach that made you stop and look, the way it rested on the knobs of her pelvis, like an egg held between the tips of two fingers.

'Roll over in the bed,' Deeds said, when he saw her rushing towards the fire. But Jammy didn't need to be told. She made him nervous. When Minnie and Binty were in the shelters drinking bottles of Buckfast Tonic Wine or VP sherry, Minnie would complain about her kidneys and then she'd go outside the shelter and squat. When she got up there would be a small pool of old woman's piss on the ground. Jammy couldn't get over it. Every time she did it he'd meet your eye in the darkness.

Minnie warmed her hands at the fire without looking at any of us. Deeds just shrugged and kept on drinking. Jammy moved round to the other side of the fire. When I looked up again I saw Binty standing just outside the firelight, his eyes squinting at us along the length of his big nose as if it was a brass telescope.

'How's Binty?' Deeds asked.

'Not the worst,' Binty said, moving closer to the fire.

'Youse must have been having a wee bit of a court up in the shelter there,' Deeds said.

'Did you slip her one?' Jammy asked.

'Pups,' Minnie said. 'I'd warm your arses so I would.'

She got up from the fire and walked away. Then she sat down in the sand and started to run handfuls of it through her fingers.

'Don't mind her,' Binty said, 'she's not well in herself these days.'

'You don't fool us,' Deeds said.

'We know what you were up to,' Jammy said. Binty shook his head and sat down beside Deeds. Deeds passed him the bottle.

We sat there for a few hours. When the vodka was finished Binty went to the shelter and brought back a bottle of Buckfast. Jammy collected more wood from the beach and put it on the fire. There must have been tar on some of the wood because through the sweet smell of the driftwood there was the black, rubber smell of tar burning.

Binty told us how the Glennons used to own a mill just outside the town. He said there was a canal which they used to take cargo from the mill. Ocean-going ships went up the canal and it looked as if they were sailing on dry land in some mystical way. The workers went out to the mill by tram and in the evenings Binty stood at the bottom of the street where the tramlines ended, selling silk stockings to the millgirls when they came off the trams, letting them run the material through their wishing fingers, pitted and black from needles and chemicals.

But there was no sign of a mill or a canal now if they ever existed. Just the fire on the rim of Deeds' glasses and

Binty's watchful talk about silk as smooth as glass that wouldn't run, how women loved it next to the skin and Deeds putting in something about how silkworms had eleven brains and Binty explaining how they boiled the worms to get the silk from them.

The glamour of thousands of tiny mouths chewing leaves, then silenced into pulpy corpses. I couldn't see it. All I could hear was Minnie's mumbling.

'The town's rotten, rotten drink, rotten men, rotten money.'

In the end Deeds stood up.

'Are you right,' he said, 'the old biddy's yap is getting on my nerves.'

We crossed the Esplanade and walked up the Harbour road until we reached Mill Street where we turned right. There was me, Deeds and Jammy and we were all wearing white tartan scarves which was Deeds' idea.

There were cars lined up along the kerb on either side of Mill Street. I don't know what it is about this town, the way they sit in cars on a Friday or Saturday night. There could be three or four people in each car or there could be none. Every so often a match strikes to light a cigarette and you can see that area of shadow between the lips and the eyes. Later perhaps a hand crosses between the seats, the shadows meet. There is a catch in the breath under the shadows.

That's not all. When it gets late they start to drive around the town. They all seem to pull away from the kerb at the same time so maybe the striking of matches is some kind of language. I don't know.

They drive slowly down Mill Street, slowly down the Harbour road. One after another they circle the Harbour and come back up the Harbour road again, taking turns to pull off into the Esplanade car park. Sometimes they keep it up all night, those darkened cargoes wheeling on some interior axis you know nothing about.

Cupid's is at the end of Mill Street, opposite the Avenue. It used to be a cinema and there is still the white plastic sign over the door where they displayed the name of the film. But that has a big, red Cupid on it now. After it was a cinema it was a woodstore before they turned it into a disco and if you looked inside it during the day it looked monochrome and smelled of sap.

But that night it was hot inside, the air inhabited all the way up to the roof. You get a look at a face turned in the light, or a breast or a leg. Before long you can't recognize anybody. Places like that make you think of fires and bodies piled at the exit.

I drank a half-bottle with Deeds on the edge of the dance-floor. Jammy looked sick. He sat against the wall with his head in his hands.

Deeds got up to dance with Anne-Marie. After a while I saw that he had his arms around her and that they were moving very slowly. As I watched his hand dropped to where the ultra-violet light made her panties show white through her trousers.

Jammy got up and walked towards the toilets. I watched him go so that I didn't see the girl until she was standing in front of me. She was wearing Wranglers and a white blouse with no sleeves. Her hair was cropped and even in that light you could see her skin was fine so that it looked as if there were blue shadows under it. When I danced with her I saw a Union Jack tattooed on her left arm above the elbow. She didn't look at me when she danced but I felt her breath on my ear and her words like some distant, incomprehensible radio station when you recognize just one word, and before I had a chance to answer Deeds was beside me telling me that Jammy had got a hiding in the bogs.

There were cubicles along one wall of the toilets and urinals on the other. There were sinks beside the urinals with specked mirrors above them. The light came from two bulbs. The reflection from the smeared blue tiles and the white porcelain hurt your eyes.

Deeds had found Jammy lying under the sinks. The floor around him was covered with wet scraps of paper towel from the plastic bin. There were red marks on his face, and some blood. When we lifted him to his feet his head yawned back and forward. Then he put his forehead against the wall and started to throw up, the vomit making a loose sound on the floor.

We took Jammy out of the toilets and got him as far as the hallway behind the main door. Anne-Marie was there. She wet a tissue, making a squirting sound with her lips, then she used it to clean Jammy's face. We started to move

19

towards the exit. There was a crowd of Prods around the door. One of them stepped forward as we were going out. His name was Glennon. He was tall with a big spade-shaped head.

'Got the message?' he said.

'What fucking message?' Deeds said.

Glennon nodded at Jammy. I kept my eyes on the black and white tiles on the floor. I was ready. Deeds stopped walking and faced Glennon. Before either of them could move the girl with the cropped hair stepped in between them, putting her arm around Glennon's waist and making him turn away.

'Your sort aren't welcome here, that's the fucking message,' Glennon said as we pushed through the doors. I looked at Deeds. Glennon's father owned most of the town and there wasn't much you could do about him but I knew Deeds would have different ideas. That came later.

I heard the door swing open behind me. It was the girl with the cropped hair. She looked at Jammy and then she looked at the rest of us.

'I hope you're proud of yourselves,' she said, 'people are only trying to enjoy themselves and the likes of you only want to spoil it.'

'We didn't start anything,' Deeds said.

'You think you're smart,' she said, 'you just go looking for trouble.'

Deeds didn't say anything. He started to walk off down Mill Street holding Jammy by the arm. Anne-Marie took

the other arm. I watched them go. Then I turned around
to look at her again. I had been right the first time. The
pupils of her eyes were almost black, like beads of hot tar.

'What do you want?' she said.

'Nothing.'

'Well what are you hanging around here for?'

'Nothing.'

'Nothing,' she said, 'Mr Nothing.' She walked to the
door and cupped her hands to look through the mesh of
the reinforced glass. Then she came back.

'All right,' she said, 'come on if you're coming.'

She was quiet until we reached the entrance to the
Avenue. She took my arm there.

'What's your name?' I asked.

'Sharon, Shazz the Razz.' She laughed, moving closer and
starting to talk. I knew why she wanted to talk. The Avenue
after Cupid's was like a field hospital at night. Couples
behind each tree, breathing in the dark, sometimes a voice,
patients talking in their sleep out of drugged pain.

She worked in the Plant. Mostly filleting dead fish that
came in frozen slabs from the big Polish boats, handbags
of guts looted and dumped. Sometimes there would be a
cargo of prawns to be shelled that would crackle and stab
the hands and leave them bleeding.

Half the girls in the town worked at the Plant, their soft,
tissue hats the only virtue in the wet and cold civilization of
fish.

Then she stopped talking and pushed me back against

a tree, kissing me so hard that our teeth met and the feeling of it went right back into my skull.

'I always wanted somebody like you,' she said. I was surprised.

When I pulled her down to the ground she came as if she had no weight but she twisted at the last moment so that I was on my back and she was on top of me. I felt her hands on my face, locating it in the dark. I put my hand on her breast. Through her blouse I could feel the jagged fringe of lace on her bra. I moved my hand down where it was softer. She put her hand on my neck. I rotated her nipple with my thumb. When I couldn't breathe any more I put my other hand to her face and found the loop of her earring in the soft, blue place under the line of her jaw. I kept pressure on it until I thought her ear would tear. Her mouth came down to meet mine then, and I could breathe again.

When it was over she sat with her back to a tree, legs drawn up to her buttocks. I gave her a cigarette and we smoked.

'You're a Taig,' she said. I didn't say anything. I knew she was a Prod the first time I saw her.

'They'll kill me,' she said, 'I don't care.' Through the trees I thought I could see the lights of cars on the Harbour road. I heard the noise of engines starting as if her words had been the signal.

Four

Deeds nudged soft blue chalk on to the tip of the cue and stood back from the table.

'She's as black as your boot,' he said, putting his hand flat on the rubbed green felt of the table, the cue running between the knuckles of his thumb and forefinger.

'The da's a reserve cop. The whole family's in it, lock, stock and barrel. UDR, RUC, you name it.'

'Prods,' Jammy said.

'So what?' I said, 'Play the ball.'

'No skin off my nose,' Deeds said.

'Did you get the tit,' Jammy said. He was standing in the corner with his hands padding the big buttons of the poker machine.

'You'll get another split lip if you don't mind yourself,' Deeds said.

A yellow went down in the middle pocket but the slope of the table carried the white ball into the bottom corner. I took the cue.

'Don't worry about it,' I said.

'Stop the lights,' Jammy said, 'it's the Scout.'

We looked into the main part of the café. You could see

his face against the window, his hand scraping a ragged seam in the streaked dirt on the outside of the glass.

'Shite,' Deeds said, 'he's coming in.'

I had my back to the door when he came in but I knew who it was. It was the same every time. He was about the town all hours of the day and night. You never knew where he would be next but every time you passed him in the dark you wondered if you'd dreamed that sick feeling that left you sweating like old cheese.

When I looked again he was standing in the doorway of the poolroom, one hand in his pocket, the other paralysed in a black leather glove and tapping his trouser leg.

They said he didn't sleep and you could believe it. If you lived in this town you carried those eyes with you. One good eye looking through you and the other one bulging from the socket, tilted and useless. No matter how tightly you drew the curtains you couldn't keep those eyes out. At night he'd be watching up the Avenue or down behind the coastguard station. In the morning you saw him in the Desmesne maybe, watching women's clothes on the washing-lines, giggling at the way they dived and swooped like turtles on the Gulf Stream and rubbing himself through the lining of his pocket until a stain the shape and colour of a copper coin appeared on the front of his trousers.

'My wee angels,' he said, looking at us. I watched his mouth. It looked as if his lips were stuck together with all sorts of things. Lint, grease, feathers. He had a sick mouth.

'I hear young Deeds got the leg over the Hicks girl last night. That's a man's work so that is. There's not many come away scot free from that. There's a quare lonely place up inside that one. I'd mind she doesn't trap you. I seen that too.'

'Seen what?' Jammy asked.

'I seen it happen. Are you trying to take a hand out of me, young Jammy, because if you are I'm fit for you.'

Jammy drew back, all eyes, and shook his head. The Scout stared at him.

'Hold your horses,' he said, 'I won't eat you yet. I'm telling you what I seen. I seen your baldy master Boyle up to the hilt one night in the back of the car and she got a hold of him and wouldn't let go. The fanny muscles lock up. Fit to be tied, so he was, with all her sweetness and her spit running down his chops.'

'Your misdeeds will be the death of me,' Jammy said and giggled.

All the time the Scout was talking his gloved hand plucked at his trousers, raising the material in tufts.

'I'll say nothing about you,' he said, looking at me. I held his eye, looking into its dark pupil, cupped in a bowl of white that was streaked with estuaries of veins.

'Mad in the head,' Deeds said.

'One eye looking at you and the other looking for you,' Jammy said.

I looked again and saw the Scout's back as the door closed behind him.

'Are you going to stand there all day,' Deeds said, 'or are you going to take that shot?'

Afterwards we went to the loft to feed the birds. To get

to it you had to go down behind the houses on the Harbour road and cross the river, jumping from stone to stone. There was a gap in the wall between the warehouse and the water and you could climb through. There was old machinery in the yard in front of the warehouse. Winches and engines soldered together with rust. Going up the ladder you could see into the big empty windows. The air coming out of them smelt of rotting sacks and bonemeal even though it was a long time since they kept anything in there, and all the floors had fallen through so that it was hollow and brown like a tooth.

Binty said that Albert Glennon owned the warehouse and that it had belonged to the Mill.

When we got to the roof Deeds took one pigeon in his cupped hands as if it was water and threw it up into the air so that you thought he had spilled it, until you heard the clap of wings on air like soft valves opening and shutting.

'We're going to race them,' Deeds said, 'me and Jammy.'

He went back into the loft. I sat on the edge of the roof. There was smoke over the roofs of the town and mist on the river. Down the street I saw Binty come out of the off-licence and sit in a doorway, looking across the street as if dreams of millgirls were walking on the opposite pavement, passing into invisibility. It was quiet, and I heard sparrows in the evening between the black, geometric telephone wires.

Five

I saw a film star on TV who said that she tried to walk as
if she was carrying a small coin between her buttocks. I
thought about that when I saw Sharon coming up the
Harbour road wearing flat shoes and a white acrylic skirt
with fish blood on it and walking as if she was wearing
high heels and carrying a coin between her buttocks or
something moister and more private like a pigeon's egg
between her thighs.

I knew that her shift ended at five so I had waited at
the top of the Harbour road until the horn went at the
Plant. Even if I had known what Deeds was planning for
the next day I would still have waited.

All the girls leaving the factory had the same
white acrylic skirts and tissue hats but some of them
were wearing jackets or cardigans over their uniforms. They
left the Plant in groups which thinned out as they got
towards the top of the hill. She was walking on her
own. She didn't stop walking when she saw me. I took
her arm.

'What do you want?'

'Nothing.'

'You're not wise,' she said and smiled. 'Look,' she said quickly, 'you know our park?' I nodded.

'Wait on the corner of it around eleven tonight. Mind nobody sees you.'

'Shazz the Razz,' I said.

'That's right,' she said, and leaned towards me, putting her mouth next to my cheek. The bite left two tiny foot-prints in the skin that wouldn't have faded completely by the time the whole thing was over. I watched her walk away, the wind pushing her skirt against the back of her knees and the dark creases there.

There were streetlights everywhere in the Desmesne. Orange lozenges floating in the damp air. I stepped back into the doorway of a garage and wondered which house was Sharon's. They all had the same roofs with red asbestos tiles and big windows blank with curtains or with light curling round the slats of venetian blinds.

She came around the back of the house opposite me and stood beside me in the doorway, not touching. I remem-bered the ultra-violet light in Cupid's, Deeds' hand placed on Anne-Marie's buttocks and the white of her panties shining through. I wondered how the light had escaped picking out the white bones on Sharon's face, the unimagin-able lingerie of death.

She led me around the back of the houses, where I followed her over a wall made of breezeblocks and into a back garden. There was a washing-line in the garden, a tricycle and a shrunken, plastic football. There was a bucket of cinders at the back door to avoid. A bedroom window was open and we climbed in through it.

And when we were in the room there was a mirror, a dressing table with bottles, the smell of her. I picked up a bottle and smelled it. She took a nightdress from beneath a pillow and undressed under it.

She got into bed. I lifted the nightdress over her breasts and smelled her private warmth. When I tried to pull it over her head she stopped me. Her nipples were hard, squeezed into pellets, and she got on top of me. After that we didn't kiss. I could feel her head against my cheek and her lips moving when she spoke her brief language into the pillow.

I climbed out of the window into a grey light which was mist by the time I reached the Banks.

The tide was out, exposing old cars and rusting tangles of steel cable. Further out the seabed must have been covered in rotting and leaking pieces of metal. Old exhausts, winches, bones, television sets. You could see the long concrete outline of the sewer outlet. If you walked to the end of it at low tide you could see where the water turned red with the effluent from McConville's slaughter yard. Sometimes plastic tampon holders came out of the end of the pipe in flocks, like birds paddling out to sea on tiny, pink feet.

You could nearly believe there was a submarine out there, trapped under the weight of blood and iron. I lit a cigarette. My eyes felt gritty, my balls were a warm sore parcel. Binty came out of the shelter stretching, and stood beside me.

'If this was Australia,' he said after a while, 'that would be a sunset out there.'

Minnie came out of the shelter after him. She stood on the other side.

'Like a great big bloody egg,' she said.

'What is?'

'The sun,' she said, pointing through the mist.

Six

That afternoon I met Deeds and Jammy in the Submarine.
It was Saturday and there were more people than usual in
the café. When I shut my eyes voices disappeared into
exhausted static, a slab of cod in hot fat like hair burning,
the hot spout of the coffee machine muzzled in cold milk.

Anne-Marie was carrying plates of half-eaten chips and
ketchup back to the kitchen.

We took a table in the corner. Jammy spilled salt on to
the table and traced his name in it. Deeds sat with his
chair tilted on to its back legs, picking threads from the
cuff of his jacket with one hand while the other cupped a
cigarette and smoked it into a tight duck's arse. Deeds had
told me about the ambush so I wasn't surprised when I
saw JB and Haresy come in through the door and look
around for us.

Haresy was called that because of his face, but it wasn't
a hare lip. He had been hit with a bottle. The split lip was
badly stitched and the nose was knocked sideways.

They came from the Chalk City, which was an old hous-
ing estate out beyond Cupid's. The houses were white going
grey with brickwork showing in places where the plaster

had collapsed. The thin hedges between the houses were broken and trampled, and the roadway was blocked by old cars, sumps and exhausts hanging out. There was a shop with heavy wire mesh over its windows and a sheet of metal on the door. At night it was dark in the Chalk City because the bulbs of the streetlights had been broken and their lead cables stripped.

You imagined that Haresy gnawed his way out of the Chalk City every so often with his torn lips hanging round his yellow teeth and JB came with him like a ghost because even though he was so big he was smooth-skinned and silent, so that you hardly knew he was there.

Haresy and JB ordered tea. When they finished it we walked to the top of the Harbour road. Deeds stood in a doorway and the rest of us crouched behind a wall. We waited for a long time. I remember JB turning to me and remarking how cold it was.

After another length of time we heard Deeds whistle. It was the signal, and the rest of them turned to look at me. I looked down and saw a beetle climbing over a leaf. Before I had finished the beetle came out from underneath. I flipped the leaf again and climbed the wall with the rest of them behind me.

It worked so that Glennon was trapped half-way between Deeds, who had stepped out from behind the doorway, and the rest of us. Glennon looked at Deeds, then looked back at the rest of us and stopped walking. He took his hands out of his pockets and left them swinging by his sides.

Deeds walked right up to him and hesitated, wanting Glennon to strike first, but he didn't, so Deeds turned sideways to him, swivelled on one foot and kicked him hard in the crotch with the other. Glennon took two steps backwards, cradling his balls but not saying anything. Then Deeds swung his fist.

It was a quiet winter's day going on towards evening. Everything was slate-grey and very still. There was the sound that an apple makes when you pull the two halves apart. Glennon went down with blood on his mouth.

It was counterfeit and we all knew it. I started to see faces, photographs, men behind barbed wire, a woman with a child on her hip and flies on her eyes, a man watching a plume of smoke rising from hills that weren't far enough away. Mortals. I wanted to know what we were doing there.

Deeds just stood looking at the body on the ground as if it were a crack that had opened in the pavement. Then he turned and walked past us as if we were invisible.

Afterwards Deeds said that he felt as if he had suddenly lost touch with everything. Not that anything had changed but that he himself had become unreal, like a ghost. I looked at him and laughed, but he didn't.

We went back to the Submarine but nobody had anything much to say. Deeds and Jammy went to the loft and the others drifted home. I sat in the Submarine until it closed. Then I walked down the Harbour road to the Banks. The sea was churning at the base of the cliffs so that it looked like the washed-out remains of a fire. I saw the

Scout coming but I stayed where I was, watching him, the way he moved, stepping out with one foot and lifting the other side of his body with a kind of shrug to get the stiff leg forward.

I thought he hadn't seen me until he stopped, the leather glove rattling against his leg with a sound like black sticks breaking. Then he was beside me, rocking backwards and forwards on his heels so that you felt somehow he was still walking through streets and estates at night, and you wanted to tell people to turn out the light before they undressed and then to lie in bed side by side without moving or even breathing, but they don't and you're watching and hearing all the small sad cries of fear and perhaps of death.

'Put four walls around it,' the Scout said, moving his good hand so that it took in the whole town, 'and a roof over it, and you'd have the biggest whorehouse in the world.'

Then he was gone again. I looked at the town. He might have been right, but the way I saw it at that moment the whole town might have gone missing so that there was nothing between the streetlights.

I started back up the Harbour road. At one place the road was narrow where the red brick houses backed on to the river. The houses had no hallway between the street and the living room so that when I looked in through one open door I saw a television set in the corner. It must have been showing the news because there were pictures of soldiers with tanks on sunlit streets that ran between small, white houses and there were children standing around, so that you wondered if somewhere off those dusty streets there were trees with real oranges on them.

Seven

But then Deeds would say that there were always wars and things going on all over the world. You just had to get used to it. Like you'd be sitting in the Submarine and there'd be a famine in Africa. No matter what you're doing, it's happening everywhere. Two people are getting in or out of bed with each other, humping and grunting. Noises you can't drown out. In beds, cars, cinemas, pavements even, all those different languages. And when you reach over to flick your cigarette into the ashtray or something like that there are women screaming giving birth and people dying in rooms as the curtains glide together until they're shut, with light and noise in the street outside, and no one has the strength to open their mouths to let out the sound of their breathing.

A few weeks after the fight with Glennon I was down at the Banks. Deeds was with Anne-Marie and there was no sign of Jammy except for the embers of a fire which had been lit earlier against the wall of the toilets. Binty sat on a piece of timber at one side of the fire and I sat at the other side. He was telling me how he had seen a dogfight over the Harbour once. It was a Sunday and people used to walk at the Harbour on a Sunday afternoon. The two planes were up there for a long time. Then one spouted a trail of black smoke and turned its nose towards the sea. They all saw the parachute open and drift towards the shingle beach below the Banks. The wind pulled the dead pilot over the shingle and his heels made a clicking noise on the stones.

'Hundreds of yards of pure silk,' Binty said, 'and your man in the middle of it.'

I heard a scuffle in the sand outside the firelight and I looked up. Sharon was standing there, breathing hard. Binty got to his feet and offered her the piece of timber but she shook her head without looking at him.

'Fancy a walk around the Harbour?' she asked me. I got up from the fire. Binty was looking straight at her.

'You'll freeze without a jacket,' he said, 'stay by the fire.' She was wearing the same blouse as she had been wearing in Cupid's. She shook her head again. I took my jacket off and she put it around her shoulders. Binty put his hand on my arm.

'Mind yourselves,' he said quietly.

I didn't say anything immediately. We walked quickly along the Banks towards the Harbour and came out behind the coastguard station where you could see the glow of radar screens behind the windows and a man's head, detecting lost objects circulating in the dark.

'What's eating you?' I asked.

'Nothing,' she said.

'Where were you going with no coat?' I asked.

'Nowhere,' she said.

'Nowhere,' I said, 'Mrs Nowhere.'

'I'm not in the mood,' she said, breaking away from me and sliding down the slope beside the coastguard station. I followed her down the slope and through the tangle of old cable and broken fishboxes at the bottom. She went along the back of the Plant. There was a brightly lit compound there, with lorry trailers parked in rows, the refrigerator units at the back of the trailers making a low sound that you could hear from a distance.

She went around the edge of the compound and came out on the other side at a place where the fence was in shadow. I saw her pull her skirt up to her waist to climb the green spiked fence. She didn't wait on the other side. I got over quickly and went after her, across a small patch of grass and then on to a concrete path which was slippery where frost spilled like the cold nitrates in the heart of stone. She stopped at a low concrete building attached to one side of the Plant. There were small windows at shoulder height. One of them was broken. She slipped her hand through the broken pane to undo the catch then she pulled herself on to the sill and wriggled through. As I followed her through the window I heard her say 'upsadaisy' from inside and giggle. On the other side the floor was wet so that your feet mewed on it when you walked. It was dark but there was a light coming from a doorway so that you could see the white bird shapes of urinals.

She called me from the door, softly, like someone keeping

a secret. She took my hand and we went out into a corridor which was like a school corridor with doors opening off it. There were globe lights hanging from the ceiling. It felt hollow walking along there with those lights crawling on the ceiling like big moths.

Outside, on the Banks, it couldn't have taken very long, kicking Binty on the ground until his loose and broken bones started to slick around under his skin. You imagine that nothing was said, that both of them were intent, Binty intent and holding his breath until a solid kick that forced the other's breath out forced Binty's breath out from between his lips as well, the two of them making a brief language that could not be heard.

The corridor led to the section of the Plant where the filleting was done. There was a time clock on the wall inside the door of the filleting section with overalls hanging on pegs beside it. The light came from fluorescent strips attached to the roof girders. I saw the place where she worked. There was a slab of wood in front of a conveyor belt with a stand beside it. There were more slabs and stands on either side of the conveyor belt.

You put a box of fish on the stand, she said. You put a fish on the slab and lifted the knife with a blade which had been sharpened so often that it had become thin and almost transparent towards the edge. The swim bladder, stomach, lungs and all the other organs came out easily. Then you fold the two sides of the fish outwards like wings and put it on the conveyor belt.

I heard a siren, and it was about that time that Jammy

had come back to the Banks and had seen the disturbed earth at the edge of the cliff and Binty face down in the builders' rubble, grass clippings and old bottles at the bottom of the cliff and had run to the coastguard station to phone, hardly able to get the words out.

Sharon was standing in front of the slab with the knife in her hand, looking at the blade.

'Do you know what I'd do if you ever two-timed me?' she said, 'I'd cut your balls off.'

I walked across the wet floor and put my hands on her breasts from behind. She put the knife down and turned to face me. We were like that for a while, struggling, then she pushed me away.

'I need a pee,' she said.

When they were lifting Binty out of the ambulance at the hospital we walked along the corridor with the moth lights back to the toilets. Sharon pushed a cubicle door open with her foot.

'Don't look,' she said. I stood in the darkness while she stripped and squatted in a single movement. After a pause the rainy whistle of her urine sounded in the bowl while deft nurse's fingers undid Binty's buttons. He was hard to handle, slippery, with bones hinged lightly in unexpected places, so they started to cut through his shirt and trousers with big shears because even though he was dead they had to look, the shears rustling and even the nurses growing silent, as if they expected to find wings neatly folded over the shoulderblades when in fact they saw an old man's body which is whiter than any silk which is worn next to the skin.

I listened to the sound of water for a long time until her bowels halted with a fledgling rustle, when I heard footsteps on the corridor outside.

I looked at Sharon. Her eyes were closed and her lips were apart.

'Heaven,' she said softly, 'heaven.'

Eight

It rained for a day and a night. The funeral took place in the rain so that Minnie's veil was stuck to her face and the yellow clay of the grave looked slick and waxy. I don't know where she got the veil. It was just a scrap of lace pinned to the front of her hair.

Everyone said it was an accident. They stood with umbrellas in the new graveyard outside the town saying it was an accident while flowers in plastic domes pushed up through the coloured stone chippings on the graves like transparent, dead foreheads.

Minnie was standing behind us at the graveside. Deeds whispered that she smelt like a brewery and Jammy started to laugh. They began to lower the coffin into the grave but just before it touched the bottom I saw soil starting to peel off the sides of the grave and then the sides collapsed and water started to pour in scattering fist-sized lumps of the yellow clay on the lid of the coffin. Nothing happened for a moment but you could see that the grave was filling with water and then the coffin began to rise again, floating on the water and bumping gently.

The water poured into the grave. It looked as if it was

never going to stop and the coffin would float over the lip of the grave, out of the graveyard, past Cupid's and the Avenue and the warehouses and the Plant, through the Harbour mouth and into the open sea.

In the end they had to lift the coffin out of the grave again and bring in a diesel pump to drain it. The pump could be heard late into the night and when it stopped there was the sound of shovels.

After the funeral we went back to the Submarine. Haresy was in the pool room with a basket that Jammy had given him to look after during the funeral. Jammy opened the basket. There was a sick pigeon in it, lying on the floor with its legs curled up. Its eyes were dull and soupy. It didn't move much except for every so often, when it would put its beak down into its breastfeathers as if it was going to preen itself – but the beak would just go into the feathers and stick there without moving. Jammy tried to give it some bread but it wouldn't take it.

Anne-Marie came into the room to wipe tables.

'I'd ride the arse off that,' Haresy said so that she could hear, but she didn't say anything or even look at him.

'Watch,' Deeds said. He went over to her and backed her against the wall, putting his hand on her cunt through the nylon apron. She didn't try to push him away. Her hands were hovering at the level of his shoulders like pink amputated nubs. I looked into her eyes and there was nothing there. Jammy and Haresy laughed.

'No flies on our Deeds,' Jammy said. Deeds tried to kiss

her but she turned her head away. The woman who owned the café came into the room and saw what was happening.

'Quit your codding around,' she said, pointing at Deeds, 'one of these days you'll go too far, son.' Deeds dropped his hands and Anne-Marie began to wipe tables as if nothing had happened.

'Fuck this,' he said, 'I'm going to the Banks.'

It was the first time any of us had been back since Binty's death. There was yellow incident tape around the broken piece of bank and a police Land Rover on the Esplanade with its engine running.

You never looked directly at those Land Rovers. You knew there was somebody behind those narrow, bulletproof windows watching you like everything else in the town. You imagined the metal and loneliness of the interior and what it would be like if they got you inside one.

Jammy pointed at the spot where the body had been lying at the bottom of the cliff.

'Silly old bastard,' Haresy said.

'The worms have him now,' Deeds said, 'making silk while the sun shines.'

I was about to say something then. About the voices I heard that night in the factory. Sharon and me in the dark, not breathing, one voice inaudible and the other a man's voice saying how he'd fix it if the other would just keep his mouth shut and who's to say that it wasn't what it looked like anyway but that he could pull strings and they knew better than to cross him in this town when it came down to it.

But Deeds had crossed the path to the shelter and I saw him motion to me to come and look. I went over and put my head inside the door. Minnie was sitting on one of the benches. She had a bottle in her hand and her cardigan had ridden up, exposing her stomach. Jammy nudged me when he saw that brown, tight thing sitting in her lap like a big nut. She was talking to herself as if there was nobody there.

'Rotten hole, rotten fucking hole, all them men hanging about for a bit of a touch, that's all they want, you'd think they were something, Binty Quinn yapping on about how silk stockings would become your smooth calves, become your smooth calves my arse, all he's looking for is a wee grope when he feels like it same as the rest of them.'

But she knew that we were there because she turned and pulled the cardigan further up.

'Go on, have a touch,' she said, 'that's what youse all want. Touch the baby.'

She was laughing now. Jammy was looking at her belly with the blind navel and the thick, unborn knots in it and he looked as if he was about to give her a dig to make her stop.

'Youse are afraid,' she said, jeering. Suddenly Deeds got down beside her and put his big hand against her belly. His hand was cupped as if for listening. Minnie shut her eyes. She just lay there with her mouth open until Deeds got up and walked away.

'Like magic,' Deeds said quietly, and when I looked back Minnie was crying like any ordinary old woman.

'That's some gut she has on her,' Haresy said outside,

'she was up the chute and she tried to hoke the baby out with a coathanger and she blew up like a balloon. So they say anyhow.'

'You wouldn't want to believe everything you hear,' Deeds said.

We walked back towards the town to go to the off-licence. Jammy brought the pigeon back to the loft and we waited for him on the bridge which crossed the river at Mill Street.

We sat on the parapet and watched gulls fighting over fish heads which were dumped at the Plant and carried upstream by the tide. The gulls took the eyes so that all you could see was bleak sockets looking up.

'That child of Minnie's,' Haresy said, 'the one she got rid of, you'd wonder who the da was.'

'Never mind,' Deeds said, 'everybody's got their secrets.'

I watched the river going past and for some reason I thought of the people who shut their eyes when they saw the cattle trucks going past on their way to concentration camps even though they knew those miles of rail would go on jolting through their children's heads.

N i n e

Down at the Banks I watched the rain make black marks
in the sand. There was nothing else to do. Haresy had gone
home when the drink was finished. Jammy sat with his
back to the toilet wall with threads of hair being blown
across his open mouth. Deeds lay on the ground with a
bottle between his knees. The fire smoked and the wind
sometimes blew the smoke back towards us.

Other nights we would have been listening to stories
that might or might not have been true, half-remembered
plots of boats that sailed on dry land, airmen from old
wars, fine ankles and calves almost invisible under the gauze
of silk and time.

I looked up when I heard the crack of broken glass
against the wall. Deeds' hand was empty and Jammy was
staring at him.

'What did you do that for?' Jammy said.

'What's it to you anyway?' Deeds said. He got to his
feet. The firelight made bright spools in the lens of
his glasses. He aimed a kick at Jammy's head but his foot
slipped in the sand and he landed on his back. He didn't
move until Jammy came over and lifted him on to his feet.

They walked off across the Esplanade. Jammy supported Deeds. I could see Jammy was talking to him the way he made kissing noises when he handled a pigeon.

I had some cigarettes left and I smoked one sitting by the fire. The rain became heavier, with sleet mixed in it. The sound of the waves on the shingle was like the insect crawl of the Scout's feet. I looked back towards the door of the shelter where Minnie was sleeping but I didn't see anything.

The wet, yellow tape around the top of the Banks crackled and the voices I had heard in the Plant came back to me. I had heard the voices and listened, but when I turned around Sharon had been standing in the cubicle with her hands over her ears and after that she was frightened. The voices faded down the corridor and I made her get through the window. As soon as we had climbed over the green railings she ran away. I didn't follow her.

I finished the cigarette. By that time the rain and sleet were coming down so hard you could barely see the Harbour. In other towns and cities it would be snowing. Close to the sea you only dreamed of snow, drifting into secret places.

I remembered the open bedroom window and the nightgown lifted over her private warmth. I started walking.

When I got to Mill Street I crossed the bridge and stopped at the chip van. I was the only one there. Empty chip bags blew about my feet as I waited. It was warm under the canopy and I listened to the radio.

But when I left the canopy the rain soaked the chips and the brown paper bag fell apart in my hands so I threw it in the gutter. I was passing the place where the bus depot used to be before a car bomb was put beside it. The bomb had sent corrugated iron from the roof flying over the town like fat, tin birds. The sound of tyres and paint cans exploding had lasted all night. Now the depot was just a compound with sodium lights, guard dogs and a high wire fence, but there was a wet, burnt smell that never left the place.

It hadn't been the only bomb in the town. Six months before that there had been a bomb at the telephone exchange and the explosion made every phone in the town ring madly at three in the morning like a pond full of black frogs.

But there hadn't been any bombs for a long time. The only things left were empty spaces and those cold ovens inside the grey Land Rovers. I put my head down and pulled my collar more tightly around my neck, with the sleet going past my skin, the touch of cold and tactile angels, winged bodies with women's legs, the feathered, dexterous touch you imagine.

The car came towards me without dipping its headlights and I looked at the pavement because the light was burning my eyes. The car went past and I looked up again. Then I heard the wet slither of tyres as it did a tight, fast turn in the road behind. I started to run, but it mounted the pavement just in front of me so that I ran into it and fell across the bonnet. My knees were numb from the impact against the front wing of the car and I felt sick. I heard a hubcap fall off one of the wheels after it struck the kerb. The hubcap rolled across the road. It seemed to take a long time. From where I was lying across the bonnet I could see the headlights pointing against the wall of a shop beside the bus depot. There was only about a foot between the lights and the wall, so that you could see every detail in the texture of the plasterwork, puckers and stretches like marks on skin, crossed by white flecks of rain and sleet. I could feel the heat of the engine through the bonnet. It made me feel sleepy.

They were in no hurry but when I heard the doors of the car open I knew I had to move. I slid off the bonnet. My legs took the weight and I put my back against the metal grille which covered the windows of the shop. They came in fast with the light behind them. the first kick missed my balls, sliding up into my stomach. The second one must have gone along my ribs.

They got in close and the fists started coming. I slipped down the grille and put my chin into my collar, making them strike from above, but that didn't last long. They lifted me and threw me face down across the bonnet. I felt kicks on my legs and punches on my kidneys.

One of them pulled me off the bonnet on to the ground.

'Keep your hands off her, Taig bastard,' an unfamiliar voice said.

'Fenian get,' another one said, and then there was one

last kick in the ribs which made a noise like gristle when you cut it with a knife, so that I felt my mouth open and a sound come out of it as if it was coming out of someone else's mouth.

The doors slammed and the car reversed away from me into the road, bumping and swaying as it left the pavement. The gears raked before the driver found first and drove away.

I lay in the street for a while with the side of my face pressed against the wet pavement. I could see where the sleet melted when it hit the pavement and I could feel water flowing through my fingers and around my cheek. The water felt warm, like bathwater.

Ten

There was no light in Sharon's bedroom but there was a car with one hubcap missing parked at her front door. I stood across the street in the doorway of a garage and waited. The wind made the plastic door behind me move with a booming noise and tore at my cigarette until the tip was a hot cone an inch long. From the house beside the garage I could hear the noise of a television. You couldn't make out the words, just distant noises like you hear through the walls of a strange room when you lie awake at night. Sounds like feet on a landing or a voice calling down the stairs or the slam of a door.

My face felt as if plaster had been moulded to it and then allowed to harden. Their fists had done that and the cold hadn't helped. On the way up the Avenue I had stopped to piss and the pain in my kidneys made me feel as if every drop was blood.

I watched the venetian blinds at the front of Sharon's house. There was a light behind them but they didn't move. I stood there for over an hour, but nothing moved except for papers filled with the wind and a piece of wire hanging loosely from a telegraph pole, tapping against a metal stanchion in a way that made you think of some kind of signal like morse, in the wind that was so cold it seemed to blow between the inside of your ribs and your lungs.

When the front door of the house opened I had to use my sleeve to get rid of the tears the wind had pushed from my eyes.

Sharon's father stood in the doorway for a moment, then he stepped aside to allow somebody out of the hall. Her father was younger than I expected, with the kind of moustache you see on policemen. He was in shirtsleeves and he kept his hands in his pockets, kicking his feet softly the way you do when you're talking to somebody at the door on a cold night.

I wasn't surprised to see Glennon there but I hadn't expected his father. I recognized the black hair and the small eyes that you couldn't see for shadow. He got into the driver's seat of the car and started it. Sharon's father waved to him as he drove off.

Glennon must have said something funny because Sharon's father laughed and punched his shoulder gently. He shut the door and Glennon crossed the street, passing me with his face set against the wind and his breath streaming out behind him while I pressed back into the doorway as far as I could, trying to pull the shadow around me.

Later that night I found myself back at the Banks. I was walking along the path where you leaned sideways into the wind coming in from the sea until it dropped suddenly, leaving you without gravity on the brink, weighted the wrong way and knowing how the stones and rubble on the beach below would hurt your bones like the cold getting through the enamel to the nerves in your teeth.

I looked over the cliff. All you could see was the black water with white foam on it. The salt spray coming over the Harbour wall made my hair stick up in drenched nubs.

I was hoping for a fire at the shelter but it had gone out, although it was warm to put your hands on the stones around it. I squatted there and heard a throat being cleared, followed by the sound of a spit.

I was in no hurry to go near Minnie, and the spit sounded like something pulled up from watery, dead lungs, but I went to the other side of the shelter anyway and looked in through the small window there. There was no glass in the window so I pulled myself up to the level of the sill and looked in. At first I couldn't see or hear anything but then there was the sound that a bottle will make when it touches the ground. I wanted a drink so I went round to the doorway. When I was inside I struck a match.

Outside it was noisy but inside it was quiet except for the flush of water from the broken urinal and the ropes of spray that had started coming over the Banks to land on the roof. Minnie was sitting on the floor. I brought the match close to her face. She had her gut in her hand like some kind of famine victim and she was twitching and mumbling through her dentures.

I reached for the bottle that was sitting on the floor in

front of her. The sweetness of VP sherry gluts your throat and stomach but it's not enough to warm you. She had seen the bottle disappear and she snatched it back.

'Would you jump into my grave as quick?' she said. She belched and said pardon before she went on.

'Silk stockings would become your smooth calves,' she said softly, 'still and all I suppose there was no harm in him, not like some others I could name.'

'Who?'

She tapped her stomach with a fingernail and gave me a sly look.

'Never you mind,' she said.

I couldn't make head or tail of it. She got up and went outside the way she did all the time. I lifted the bottle and took another drink. She stood in the doorway when she came back, looking up and down, then she came back and sat down heavily beside me. Suddenly she took my hand and stuck it under her coat. I could feel the pulled greasy wool of her cardigan under my fingers and beneath that her belly, hard as a nut, with ridges in it like iron. Her nails dug into me. She had a smell like old rinds.

'The man who done that to me,' she said and I felt her hand chasing mine under the cardigan until she found it and pushed it against her stomach so hard the knuckles cracked.

I couldn't move. I felt as if she was going to burst me open against whatever secret she kept in that solid flesh.

'God, child,' she said then, 'you're foundered with the

cold.' She tightened her grip until I was pressed against her old woman's boulder stomach and scraggy tits. I remembered a night during the summer. I was standing in the car park outside Cupid's. There were other people in the car park. It was a warm night. You could have heard someone laughing from a long way.

In one corner of the car park there was a couple standing against the fence. He had his back to me and her face was almost invisible in the shadow. She was wearing a blouse with a loose neck which was pulled down at the side so that one breast was exposed.

I could see the long white gland clearly, as if it was floating on the air in front of my eyes, and as I looked I heard her laugh with a sound that filled my ears as if stars of ash were colliding a long way into space.

'Whisht,' Minnie said. 'Whisht now.' Her grip relaxed so that she was holding me the way you would hold a child. I pushed her off me. She coughed and held her stomach. Outside the wind was loud and the sea slapped like wet leather against the stones on the beach and the concrete of the pier wall.

Eleven

That week it seemed as if there was nobody in the town any more. The wind carried slates from the warehouse into the river and made noise in the aerials on the coastguard station. In the morning there were always bottles and wet solids of puke in the gutters but you never saw who left them there. Up in the Desmesne there were parties at night. You heard the noise but you never saw anyone coming or going.

Deeds said it was like a town that was expecting an invasion. Saigon, Managua, one of those names you hear on television. Anyone with anything to lose has already left quietly at night. You didn't want to be among the ones that were left behind but you were.

I said that every time I walked through the town I got the kind of feeling you have when you wake up at night suddenly and you don't know where you are so that everything is strange, and Deeds said that was right too.

The day after I got the hiding I was walking down Mill Street when I saw Deeds and Jammy on top of the loft. There was a strong east wind and you saw all sorts of things flying through the air. I saw a cloud of litter being blown towards me and in the middle of it was a woman's blouse, sleeves puffed with invisible flesh. I saw a plastic bin tumble all the way from the bridge to Cupid's. All sorts of things. When I looked up and saw Deeds and Jammy up there I almost expected to see them take off from the roof, arms spread.

I climbed the ladder and found them putting a rope over the top of the loft to hold it down. I didn't ask them where they got the rope. Maybe it came there on the wind.

'Stop the lights,' Jammy said when he saw my face.

'What happened to you?' Deeds asked.

'I was talking when I should have been listening,' I said.

'Last night?' Deeds asked. I told them what had happened.

'Should have listened to your Uncle Deeds,' Deeds said.

'No flies on our Deeds,' Jammy said.

Later Deeds asked me if I was seeing her again and I said that I didn't know. But later that evening I waited at the top of the Harbour road. When her shift ended I saw the white uniforms coming up the road in the fading light. She wasn't there.

Deeds and Jammy spent the next few days at the loft and at night Deeds brought Anne-Marie to the Avenue or up to the loft.

In the middle of the week I was standing on the corner of Mill Street and the Harbour road. I was in a shop front, out of the rain. A drainpipe emptied off the roof on to the pavement beside me, making a noise like bare feet on wet tiles.

I must have been standing there for a long time with those feet running through my head. I didn't see the car until it had stopped at the kerb in front of me. The driver was invisible, but the passenger window was open and I saw Glennon staring at me, his big pale lips and small eyes, the skin around his eyes the same colour as his lips. He smiled at me. The top lip didn't move on one side when he smiled because there was still some swelling on it from Deeds' fist. I backed into the doorway and waited for them to come at me, but Glennon just leaned his elbow on the car window and smiled.

'Now you know what happens to Taigs who go out with our girls,' he said, 'this is our town, kid, and she belongs to us. If anybody's going to throw a shot into her I will.'

I watched the car pull away from the kerb. When I took my hands out of my pockets they were scored red where the edge of the pocket had cut into my fist.

I crossed the street to the newsagent's. The man in the shop had a bottom lip which stuck out. The lip was wet and there were shreds of tobacco on it. I bought cigarettes and he counted the change on to the counter. You could see the way the bones in his hand moved to make pockets of skin. There were yellow stains on his finger and thumb. When I reached for the change he gripped my arm.

'You see days like these,' he said, 'they could be the best days of our lives.' Outside I looked towards the loft and saw Sharon climbing the ladder towards it.

There was no sign of her on the roof. I went into the loft. She didn't look around when I came in. There were pigeons all around her but she wasn't looking at them either. It was the pictures that interested her. Deeds had cut them from porn mags and stuck them to the wall of the loft. In the darkness the coloured squares of paper looked like rows of windows in which women were undressing.

'My da keeps a stack of them books in the garage,' she said. She had her hands in the front pockets of her leather jacket so that the bones of her shoulders showed through the stretched leather. Her hair was greasy and flattened on one side as if she had slept on it.

'What are you doing here?' I asked. She shrugged and turned to face me, putting her hands behind her back, palms pressed against the wall and buttocks resting on her hands. Her eyes were black and her head was tilted so that you could see the blue shadows on her throat. When I touched her she was cold under her jacket and on her mouth.

She pushed me away and asked for a cigarette. I gave it to her and lit it, watching the way her eyelids fell as she bent forward, taking the light from my cupped hands with sipping breaths. The light from the match must have shone upwards into my face because her expression changed when she looked at me. She touched my cheek.

'Bastards,' she said, 'they had to tell me what they done to you. I near tore my da's eyes out and they wouldn't let me out of the house after that. I locked myself in the bathroom tonight and done a runner out the window.'

She hesitated, dragging on the cigarette.

'I can't go back,' she said, 'I need someplace to go.'

I thought about it. She went outside and walked to the edge of the roof. It was getting dark. You could see lighted windows in the Desmesne and streetlights going down towards the Harbour.

'You can see for miles,' she said. She held her cigarette between finger and thumb as if she was sighting on a distant landmark, then she flicked it and watched it fall into the river below.

She couldn't stay at the loft but there was an old net store down at the Harbour. We climbed back down the side of the warehouse. I wondered how she had avoided Deeds' traps. Later on I found out that you only fell into Deeds' traps if you wanted to.

I bought food on the way. She had a plastic bag with clothes in it. When we got to the Harbour we went around the inner basin, past the winches they used to unload the Polish boats. After that the tarmac road ran out and you were on dirt and stones. We reached the old boatbuilder's yard. Wooden buildings with tarred roofs. It was like walking through an ancient village. You expected old women in doorways, looking up at you when you passed, opening broken mouths wordlessly.

The net store was built on wooden piles over the water. Inside there were two skylights in the roof and torn nets on the rafters. There were holes in the plank floor and through the holes you could see the water beneath the building, black and glistening from diesel spillage.

Sharon took the food out of the plastic bag and set it out on the floor. For a while all you could hear was the sound of eating.

'I was starving,' she said.

'What's the plan now?' I said. 'You can't stay here for long.'

'Don't know.'

'The roof is all right, though,' I said, 'and you can sleep on the nets. Make them up into a bed.'

'We could go away,' she said.

I pulled some nets out of the rafters and piled them in the corner nearest the door. I stretched out on them. The place smelt of tar, wood and fish, and the water smelt of oil. She was watching me. The store was dark except for the Harbour lights which came through the skylights, so that if you stared at her it seemed as if the skin was sinking between the bones on her face.

She came over and sat down beside me, then she lifted her hand and touched my face again. Perhaps she had seen the same thing there. I brought her face closer to mine. She sucked my lip into her mouth. When she put her weight on top of me I could feel debris in the net pressed into my back. Shells, sea-urchins and starfish.

I stayed all night. You could stay there forever, listening to the soft snaps and pulls of her breath, with the voices of the tide coming in underneath you, covering the mud and settling around the piles.

Twelve

You imagine the feeling people must have had when they looked up and saw an airship for the first time. That anything so big could be light enough to float, all those silent miles of air, cable, canvas and rope.

It was the same when we woke up that morning and saw a big Polish boat coming into the Harbour. I looked through a chink in the wall and all that was visible in either direction was the side of the ship. Green plates of steel and rivet heads brown with rust. You could barely tell that it was moving. There was just the sound of the engines and minute ripples at the waterline as if some small animal was digging itself into the Harbour bottom.

I went outside. The boat was taller than the Plant. They were using winches to bring it alongside the dock. As the stern swung round I could see to the other side of the inner basin. Deeds and Jammy were there. Even at that distance I knew what they were doing. They were waiting at the edge of the dock until a seagull flew past in the Harbour below them. Then they would try to bring it down with pieces of broken pallet or fishbox. They were easy to bring down. All you had to do was touch them.

I shouted across the inner basin. They waved to me and
began to walk around the basin. I told Sharon that I
wouldn't be long. I went as far as the Plant and waited for
them beside the skips of fish guts that were left at the front
of the Plant at the weekend. When the weather was hot
the skips made a boiling sound and you could smell them
all over the town.

But I heard a different kind of sound when I was standing
there. I went to the back of the skips and I saw the Scout
using his good hand to fork handfuls of the guts into a
plastic bag.

'Puts lead in your pencil,' he said, 'and you'd need that
in this town, so you would if you seen the things I seen.'

'What did you see?' Deeds asked as he walked up.

'Up in them new houses I seen things,' the Scout said,
'up in the Desmesne, nudie women running around all
week.'

'Don't talk shit,' Deeds said.

'I seen it. Men with no faces.'

'You're having us on,' Deeds said.

'I've seen it,' the Scout said, 'they put sheets across the
middle of the room with holes in them and the men put
their dicks through the holes and the women pick and
choose, squealing like pigs at the market. Men with no
faces.'

It wasn't the kind of market I imagined. I could see
women moving among the secret stalls, handling the
merchandise, blind roots, tubers of bliss.

Jammy giggled and the Scout put his head back and laughed so hard that you could see the back of his throat. His sick laugh. I could see the way he was holding the plastic bag, twisting it, his good hand working at the neck in a way that made me uneasy, and the others must have noticed it as well because Jammy stopped giggling and Deeds' eyes narrowed.

'We're no angels, are we, boys?' The Scout's voice was like a hand on your throat and Deeds stepped forward with his fists clenched.

'Hard men,' the Scout said, 'hard as whores' handbags.'

Deeds looked at me. Nobody was laughing. The Scout held up the dripping plastic bag.

'None of youse joining me for a wee bite of dinner?'

He was gone then. You never knew how he could move so quickly.

'He's not the full shilling, yon boy,' Jammy said.

We started to walk back towards the head of the inner basin where the river emptied into the Harbour. The tide was out and Jammy lobbed stones at bottles trapped in the black mud on the Harbour bottom. There was a smell like burnt rubber from the mud. Sometimes the stone would hit the iron pilings which supported the side of the dock, making a dull ring like a spoon on the side of a cup. Other times the stone would land in the mud, making a clean, triangular hole, darker than the surrounding mud.

When we reached the head of the basin we climbed down a concrete bank on to the riverbed. There was room to walk along the edge without stepping into the water until you reached the place where the concrete ended. Then there were two fields which were marked off for building land, and you could walk through the fields until you reached the warehouses. There were trees overhanging the water, with dried weed and plastic bags in their lower branches from floods. On the other side of the river you could see the backs of houses on the Harbour road. When the river flooded the water could rise to the level of the back windows and deposit parcels of mud and silt smelling of meat in ground-floor rooms. But that hadn't happened for a long time.

Further up the river there was a place where the water had cut away a high bank, leaving a small cliff with a tree on top. One of the branches of the tree jutted out over the river and there was a rope attached to it.

I went up first. I took my jacket off and used it to lasso the rope. There was a knot at the end of the rope and I put one foot on the knot and pushed with the other so that I went spinning out over the river fifty feet below.

At the arc of the swing you could see all the way down the river to the Harbour. You could see all the roofs, gutters and gables of the town. You could see the silver roof of the Plant and you could see the new, grey roofs of the houses in the Desmesne. You could see towns without people, or with people so small they were only the size of a fingernail.

The rope rotated so that I could see down between the red brick houses on the Harbour road where the pavement wasn't wide enough to wheel a pram. The wind had subsided during the night and the air was still. There was smoke from chimneys hanging in the air between the houses. Some children were pulling a bogey made of an old fishbox and bicycle wheels along the road. The fishbox contained lemonade bottles half filled with silt. The children found them in the river and brought them back to the shop for the deposit. Further on down the road the pavement was chalked off for hopscotch and some girls were bouncing a tennis ball off a gable and singing.

I could make out the Submarine as well. Anne-Marie was outside washing the windows. She had a plastic bucket and a cloth. When she lifted her arm out of the bucket it was red and steaming because of the cold air. When she reached towards the glass it was as if I could see along the white underside of her arm to the wet curled darkness of her armpit. Every time her arm passed over the glass I could feel the soft grunt she made in the back of her throat.

I was getting tired. If you didn't keep enough momentum going on the swing it slowed down until eventually you couldn't step back on to the top of the cliff. If that happened the only thing you could do was to hold on until you couldn't hold on any longer and then just drop off into the river below where the water was shallow.

I got off on to the bank and Deeds got on. Deeds could swing higher than any of us. He stayed up there for a long time, jack-knifing on the rope, the rope coughing against the branch, his body making the sound of wings as it went through the air, swinging higher than the rest of us, until he could see on to the roof of the warehouse where the door of the loft was unlocked when it shouldn't be and was swinging backwards and forwards in a breeze which you couldn't feel at ground level, opening and closing on a doorway as dark as the Scout's throat.

The rope twitched as Deeds checked it at the high point of the swing, destroying the momentum so that he had to dive for the bank on the back swing, losing his footing, then picking himself up and running for the river.

We followed him, running upstream through the water, our feet slipping on the greasy rocks, the ladder on the side of the warehouse swaying under our weight, the tiles on the roof slithering.

You've seen footage of great disasters on television with the victims laid out on the floor of an aircraft hangar or school gym, covered in blankets. It was like that. The pigeons were lined up in neat rows, each one with its neck broken and a tiny bubble of dried blood on its beak. Jammy stood there with a red face and his hands in his pockets, looking down at the birds as if it was a trick where you lifted the right bird and you found a coin or a tiny, beating heart underneath.

Deeds didn't seem to look at the birds. He had the same expression on his face as he did the time he fought Glennon.

After a long time he began to lift the birds and carry them to the edge of the roof, one by one. He didn't say a word. Jammy stood at the door of the loft, watching him, then he went to the edge of the roof and looked over. He walked back to the loft, put his head against the door and started to cry.

Deeds carried all the birds to the edge. It was very quiet. All you could hear was the voices of girls playing hopscotch on the Harbour road below. And when Deeds dropped the birds off the edge of the roof their ounces of flesh and hollow bone made no noise as they fell.

Thirteen

Deeds arranged to meet Haresy and JB in the Submarine at four o'clock. We met them on the way there and went into the pool room. JB put money in the pool table and poured the pool balls, jolting, into the wooden triangle.

'So Glennon's for it,' he said. Deeds screwed the blue chalk on to the tip of his cue and rolled the white ball on to the edge of the ruined felt crescent.

'The heavy dint,' Haresy said. Anne-Marie came in and began to wipe tables. Deeds placed the sucked welt of his cigarette carefully on the rim of the table without looking at her. Outside the sky was blue, darkening as the sun went down. Frost had begun to show white on the black tarred roof of the loft by the time we came down to the ground, leaving Jammy there.

'You should have fucking done him the first time,' Haresy said, 'them birds were worth a fortune.'

'They hang around the top of the Avenue after Cupid's,' JB said, 'there's only a couple of them usually. We could do it then.'

'His own ma won't know him,' Haresy said.

'All right,' Deeds said, 'tonight.'

'Is he in on it?' Haresy said, jerking his head at me.

'Why wouldn't he?' Deeds said. Haresy didn't look in my direction.

'Things get around,' he said, 'he goes out with that wee Prod from the Desmesne, and her da hangs out with Glennon.'

'There's no law against a Prod going out with a Taig,' Deeds said.

'I seen the two of them up at the loft last night,' Haresy said.

'Wise up,' Deeds said so softly you could barely hear him.

'I hear tell them Prods ride like rabbits,' Haresy said. He laughed and walked quickly and noiselessly around the table until he was standing behind Deeds. He put his hands on Deeds' back and castored on his hips, thrusting his crotch into Deeds' buttocks.

'Black hole,' he said, 'nothing like it.' Deeds pounded the butt of the cue into his stomach and turned, holding the cue by its tip. His face was white. Haresy fell back against the wall.

'I was only messing,' he said.

'We'll meet at the Banks, at eleven tonight,' Deeds said.

Deeds went back to the loft, where Jammy was still sitting where we had left him. Wide-awake and listening to the eggs whispering to each other in their cold nests.

I thought about what Haresy had said on my way back

to the net store. I thought about Glennon wetting his lips. I thought about those grey Land Rovers, Sharon spilling her brief language on to the metal floor.

The big Polish boat filled the Harbour with lights. There was a smell of coffee. Men were moving about on the upper decks and there was music coming from somewhere.

She looked frightened when I pushed open the door of the net store. She was sitting at the far end of the building on the edge of one of those big holes in the floor. When she saw it was me she looked back down at the water. I sat down beside her.

'I was just thinking,' she said, 'you know the way you look at the water and it's the same water everywhere. Like if you went to the other side of the sea it would still be the same water.'

I knew what she meant. The same black water burning against chunks of floating ice and against coral and sandy beaches in the night.

'Like when you look at the sky,' she said, 'it's the same so it is, doesn't matter where you are in the world.'

She sounded like Binty. I told her what had happened to the pigeons.

She was sitting with her hands between her thighs and her eyes reflecting the colour of the water, returning its blackness through a hole in the world.

'Did you hear the music?' she asked.

'What?'

'The music. I listened to it all night waiting for you to

come back. I thought something had happened.'

'Why didn't you tell me that you knew what Glennon had done to Binty? You knew that he didn't fall over the Banks. You knew that Glennon did it and his da covered up.'

'Take me away from here,' she said quietly, 'I'm going to die here.'

'Tell me why?'

'You know nothing,' she shouted, 'please can we go, please?'

Every so often a car goes over the edge of the dock and into the Harbour. The last time it happened you could see the skid marks leading up to the dock and the car headlights under the water. That happens sometimes. The headlights stay on until water gets into the electrics.

I was there when they lifted the car out using a crane. There was a frogman in the water. When the car cleared the surface a lot of water ran out of it at first but by the time it got to the level of the dock there was very little.

I saw a young couple sitting upright in the front seat. The car was swinging and tilting slowly on the chains and you could hear the noise that the generator and the crane made, but everybody on the dock was very quiet, as if they could hear the silence in the car as it sat on the Harbour bottom, two pairs of eyes staring through the windscreen to where the headlights opened the darkness like a door opened on to an empty room.

We stared at the water in silence for a long time. When I got up to go I felt her touch my arm.

'I swear I never,' she said, 'I swear.'

But she didn't go on. Outside I zipped up my jacket. I had forgotten how cold it was.

Fourteen

I recognized the car that was parked in the Esplanade car park. My knees had left shallow dents in the front wing. I put my hand on the bonnet where the lacquer was warm and smooth.

I recognized the voice that had spoken in the Plant that night. Albert Glennon was on his hunkers in front of Minnie. From the doorway of the shelter I saw his hair oiled back over the skull and the scalp showing white between the black strands like dead skin, the nose and the thin lips. His eyes were sunk into shadow, or pulled into shadow like a glove pulled inside out.

'I seen him do it,' Minnie said, 'I knew him for a son of yours. He's the spit of you by the face.'

'You've a hard heart,' he said.

'Hard heart my arse, and me never saying a word this twenty-five year about the way you left me and never seen hide nor hair of you since. Mind you, I'd rather not have the child if it ended up like thon skitter, or like you. You never gave me a red cent for ripping out my insides for you.'

'Are you sure you saw him, Minnie?'

'I saw your son kicking Binty.'

'I'll say he was up at the house that night. Your word against mine, Minnie.' The man's voice was soft like bad meat.

'Aye, your word and mine. Never fear, I'll go to no police barracks telling tales about your son. Sure, who would credit me anyway? You have the law in your pocket.'

'I knew you'd see sense, Minnie. You're a sensible girl.'

I saw him change position. One of his hands held her wrist and the other rose to her face. I watched it fan there like breath. It stayed for a moment, then it dropped to her neck.

'You're a sensible girl, Minnie,' he said again. His voice was cold and hollow. I could see the broad, flat tips of his fingers and the nails coloured by the freezing, watery light in the shelter, the rubbery wattles of her neck rubbed smooth under the fingers so that you could almost hear the rustle of blood and breath in the skin. I wanted to shout out to her but I couldn't.

'Just a wee touch, Minnie,' he said, 'you're a sensible girl.'

One hand went from her neck to the opening of her cardigan. It entered quickly, disappearing into the wool. His other hand was working at his crotch. The zip slid down. It was the sound of a thousand small mouths chewing, oozing silk.

I left the shelter and didn't go back, even when Albert Glennon left, walking on to the Esplanade without looking right or left, starting his car and driving off. But once you heard the kind of noises two people make together you never forget them.

Deeds arrived alone. I started to tell him everything but I kept quiet when I realized that he wasn't listening. When I stopped talking he looked at me.

'You look like you've seen a ghost,' he said. It made me feel uneasy. He handed me a bottle of vodka and I took a long drink.

Haresy and JB arrived about five minutes later. I handed the bottle to JB. While he was drinking, Haresy took a Stanley knife out of his pocket and swung it at stomach level.

'Gut the bastard,' he said, smiling with his broken mouth. He put the knife back into his pocket. JB handed him the bottle. When he drank the liquid ran out of the corners of his mouth. Deeds looked over at me. His smile came and went like smoke.

'Come on and get it over with,' he said.

'Where's Jammy?' JB asked.

'I couldn't find him,' Deeds said.

'Who needs him?' Haresy said, touching his pocket.

It was cold. We crossed the Esplanade. You could see the lights of Mill Street up ahead.

'Looks like a border,' Deeds said, pointing at the double row of streetlights. He was thinking that we were walking towards a border without passports, wondering if you could break out, climb the barbed wire, cross the brightly lit strip without stepping on the freshly dug patches that would conceal mines. Hoping that the guards were asleep in their watchtowers, or sitting in warm guardrooms passing around snapshots of their wives, children, sweethearts.

Our feet made a snapping noise on the pavement. Behind me I could hear Haresy chafing his hands against the cold.

We turned the corner on to Mill Street. When it is cold like that, everything else is suppressed so that you can hear the silence of lifeless things in your head and see ghost shapes of cars, lamp posts and people caught in frost.

We stood behind the wall at the top of the Avenue and waited for Cupid's to end. We waited for a long time. There were no couples walking up the Avenue from Cupid's but when you had waited that long you started to imagine silent couples pinned to each tree with frost, clothes and skin stiff with it.

We heard the noises that meant Cupid's was over. Someone whispering, someone crying, a shadow of vomit on the ground.

The noises stopped. There was no sign of Glennon. Ice cracked in the branches of the trees behind us. The noise of a bird's small heart frozen in flight.

In the end Deeds straightened his legs and stood up.

'He's not coming,' he said. He lit a cigarette and shivered. Haresy and JB stood up as well. Haresy said something under his breath. JB said something back. I didn't look round. Then Haresy was in front of me, pointing his finger in my face. I had been waiting for this.

'Glennon knew about this from the start so he did,' he said. 'You fucking told him. You're hand in glove with that lot, you and your black cunt, even showed her the way to the loft.'

Haresy turned to Deeds who hadn't moved.

'He's a squealer, so he is,' he said. Deeds shook his head slowly and dragged on his cigarette. JB didn't move. Haresy looked back at me. He had his hand in his pocket. I backed out of the Avenue gates slowly and Haresy followed. The Stanley knife came out of his pocket.

'That black bitch,' he said, 'you'd eat a mile of her shite to get up her hole.'

As he came towards me I remembered the way Sharon had come to the shelter on the night Binty had been killed and how she had wanted to take me away because she must have known that Glennon was looking for one of us. She couldn't warn me. You get a habit of silence in this town.

Haresy brought the knife up from the level of his waist. I could see rust on the blade. I caught his wrist and used his own momentum to spin him around. I pushed him across the pavement in front of me with his arm forced up his back until he collided with a parked car. A wing mirror broke off its stem with a chipped sound, leaving just the chrome stem pointing upwards like a long fingernail, the cuticles stripped.

We just stood like that for a moment. Haresy was drawing long bubbling breaths through his split mouth. All I wanted to do was to get to the net store.

Haresy twisted out of my hands. I reached for him again. He jumped and landed on the bonnet of the car. I stopped moving and watched the way his feet started to slip on the bonnet which was white with frost. Through the windscreen I saw someone in the passenger seat light a cigarette. The match flared and the shadow fell between the lips and the eyes. Haresy's feet went out from under him. You could see which way he was going to fall, but it took a long time before his face dipped towards the stem of the wing mirror, his head bowed as if he was drinking. There was no sound. The bone socket of his eye fitted the metal and then there was just the chrome again, dark this time.

The next thing I remember is Deeds pulling me to my feet and forcing me to run through the gates of the Avenue. JB just looked after us and smiled. We turned off the Avenue and into the trees. Behind us I could hear Haresy shouting.

'I'm blinded, I'm fucking blinded.' We slid into the bottom of a ditch. Old bottles and plastic bags caught in frozen water crunched like bird-skulls under our feet. We climbed on to a wall and jumped down on to the other side.

It was a moment before I realized that we were in McConville's yard. There were steel pens in front of us and a long low shed beyond that. There was a single bulb on the outside of the shed and you could see where the yard sloped to a drain with an iron cover.

We walked into the middle of the yard. It was slippery

where it had been washed and the water had turned to ice. The light from the bulb was brittle. We couldn't hear Haresy any more. Our breath spilled out like soft voices into the empty pens and the shed.

Deeds went towards the shed. I saw him disappear inside the open doors. He called to me.

Inside the shed it was bright. There were only a few lights but the walls were painted white. On each side of the building there was a metal rail with meathooks every few feet. The rails went all the way to the back of the building. Under the rails there were channels cut in the concrete floor. The floor was dark and wet and the hooks were bare.

Deeds leaned forward to touch a chain which was attached to one of the hooks. The rail shook and all the hooks moved at once, heavily as if they were hung with invisible carcasses, jostling each other and dripping into the gutters.

Deeds touched the chain again and all the hooks shook their whitened tips and the shed filled with noise.

81

Fifteen

By the time I got to the net store that night I knew that it was too late. The small door at the side was open. You expect to see signs of a struggle. A door swinging on broken hinges, tables and chairs overturned, blood perhaps. But an unwashed cup or food wrappers lying on the table or clothes tangled in the pile of nets is violence enough to convince you.

I walked across to the nets. There was a black room between the floorboards and the water beneath. My feet echoed in it. I picked up a teeshirt from the pile of clothes. It smelt of nets. I found a pair of jeans with panties balled in the crotch. The panties had a comb of lace on the front and around the legs like the lips of an anemone. They were cold and stiff.

'You'll not find her in there at any rate,' the Scout said. His uneven footsteps followed me across the floor.

'She's long gone, back to daddy, I'd say.' I thought about the last time I'd seen her, hunched and frozen.

'She's warm enough,' he said. Then I imagined one of those Land Rovers drawn up outside the net store, Sharon climbing into the back, the noise the doors made as they closed and the small square of greenish bulletproof glass that you couldn't see through from the outside.

'Nobody took her,' the Scout said, 'left of her own free will so she did.' I turned to look at him and I saw what had happened. Glennon standing in the doorway of the net store. Sharon watching him in the darkness. Her feet inaudible on the floor when she joined him. She didn't look once at the Polish boat as they walked around the inner basin.

'Now there's a thing for you,' the Scout said. 'I wouldn't have believed it if I hadn't seen it with my own two eyes.'

I still had the jeans in my hand. I threw them away so that they slipped through one of the holes in the floor and fell through without noise as if they hadn't touched water but had kept on falling. When I turned the Scout had gone.

Sixteen

Deeds used to say that words leave shadows in your mind and Binty used to talk about the city where they dropped the first bomb. How people were sitting on doorsteps and walking on the pavements. The sun must have been shining. They heard planes but they didn't look up because they heard planes every day. Sparrows sat on telegraph poles and pigeons flew along the rivers, staying close to the walls on either side. The pavements were dusty, dreaming of rain. And then the stars collapsed and turned to ash. The hot wind collected the ash and took it away and there were shadows of people sitting on doorsteps, walking on the pavement. Their shadows were printed on the ground and the ashes rustled in the wind and were gone.

Jammy wasn't missed until the next day, and it was Deeds who found him, floating face up in the river downstream from the warehouses.

Everyone assumed that he had stumbled into one of Deeds' traps and the police had put incident tape across the river. I found Deeds down at the Banks.

He told me how he'd found Jammy wedged between rocks with his head pointing downstream, the current rolling it from side to side as if he was being interrogated by an invisible hand. The blood had drained from his face so that his complexion was clear, and his hair streamed out behind him. Deeds swore he looked beautiful. Then he told me that Jammy hadn't slipped. The other thing had never occurred to me.

Words leave shadows in your mind. Deeds talked so that his voice was soft like wings alighting on the tin roofs and slates and gutters and telegraph wires of the town. He told me about the first night he had brought Anne-Marie to the loft and how he had stayed on her until the whole loft shook and the pigeons were dislodged from their perches like big fruit, soft in their panic with their wings thudding against the wooden walls. They lay awake in the silence afterwards, her eyes open in the dark, a packet of Frenchies scattered on the floor glowing like silkworms and Deeds smoking with the cigarette cupped in his hand and butts stubbed out on the lid of a paint can on the floor.

Other nights Deeds would sit on his own at the edge of the roof. Sometimes, he said, the town would be noisy at night, sounds coming up from locked bedrooms as if you were on the other side of a thin wall in a strange room and heard a man's voice and then a woman's. On nights like that the lights in the Desmesne would seem to burn until morning. Sometimes it would be quiet, and he would watch the town dwindle and empty.

On a quiet night he climbed the ladder and looked into the loft. Jammy was asleep on the floor with one hand on a wicker basket which had a pigeon's beak coming out of an airhole on the side.

Deeds walked back on to the roof and stood at the edge. He told me he felt as if he could have lifted the loft without waking Jammy, put it on the palm of his hand and blown lightly, and then watched it float over the edge, going downriver towards the sea and weaving when the wind brushed it.

I wanted to know what else he had seen from the loft. You could have seen anything from there. But when I turned he was gone and I remembered what he had said about being invisible.

Seventeen

The rain began after dark. You stand at the edge of the Banks looking out at the sea and at the Harbour where the arc lights come on all at once and you wait as if you're waiting for a signal but it doesn't come, or at least not from the direction you expect.

When the rain began I turned and went back to the shelter. The rain was inside my collar and running down my back. When I got to the shelter I saw Sharon inside, hunched on one of the benches with her legs drawn up so that her heels touched the point of her buttocks and her chin rested on her knees.

It was almost as if I had suddenly seen Binty, his mouth reeling stories like silk through the dead emptiness. I stood there for a long time. She didn't look at me or say anything at first. I sat down beside her. I could feel the rain seeping through my jacket and I realized that she hadn't been there for long, because her hair was wet and when she moved her arm I saw how the material of her blouse left a shadow of water on the wall so that she would be cold to touch.

'I'm afraid,' she said.

'I know.'

'You don't know,' she said, 'you weren't there when I came back last night.'

The night that Binty was killed, she said, she was upstairs when she heard Glennon tell her father that he was going to the Banks to wait for Deeds or me. Glennon saw her and pushed her back against the wall, he dug his thumb into her eye and told her to keep her mouth shut, and her father laughed.

Then I had left her alone in the net store. Glennon found her there. He had reached it just as we were leaving the Banks to wait for him outside Cupid's.

Afterwards she lay on the nets for a long time. She could see the two cups that we had used to drink from on the first night. The shape of mouths on the rim of each obliterated by arc lights from the Harbour shining through the roof.

'He hurt me,' she said. She unbuttoned her blouse. There were braided marks on her neck and ribs. Nailmarks on her breasts. Her nipples were hard and cold like small stones.

But then it wasn't the first time she had been hurt. Those magazines her father kept in the garage. The colour pages that were still sticky when you touched them. And then you see your father and the thing you remember is that there is hair growing in his nose and ears, not that his hands are rising like water around your calves, filling the space between heartbeats, rustling in the hollows at the back of your knees.

She put her arm around my waist and her head on my chest so that I could feel the small, wet hairs on her temple and when I pressed my chin down to hold her I could detect the light, mobile bone of her skull underneath her hair. Her mouth moved against my chest. She had allowed Glennon to kiss her so that when she suggested that they go to the Plant he had followed her without question.

She kissed me again. I opened my eyes when I felt her mouth against mine. In the darkness there was the round blue bulb that her eye made under the skin of the eyelid. I had one hand on her ribs feeling her heart's noise. Her tongue was in my mouth. Flat, strong muscle stroking the ridges of my palate, her heart's fat animal of chambers and valves moving faster. I took my mouth away from hers.

'Why did you go to the Plant?' She shrugged.

'I'll show you,' she said.

When we came out from behind the coastguard station I could see the Polish boat forming a fence of lights across the Harbour. The tide was in and black water came through the narrow channel at the pier, filling the inner basin to the brim, pushing fish heads up the river, past the warehouses and the back walls of houses on the Harbour road and under the bridge. You imagined the Harbour filling until fish heads began to burst through floorboards in the town.

The rain came on the east wind across the Harbour wall to blow flat on the dock and the water. The bollards along the edge of the basin were dark and wet. There was a chip van on the edge of the dock. You could see the steam from it being blown down towards the concrete where it seemed to stop for a moment before the wind caught it again and made it disappear.

She slid down the slope behind the coastguard station, turning to urge me on when she got to the bottom, the wind making shapes in the wet material of her blouse.

I lost my footing on the slope and landed on an old fish-box which cracked and splintered under my weight but I didn't lose sight of the white blouse, the tiny, perfect organs of her shoulderblades beating inside it as she walked away.

The Plant had been closed for the weekend. The compound was full of lorry trailers that would be taken away on Monday morning. You could feel the noise of their diesel cooling units in the ground under your feet.

Sharon climbed the fence. She pulled up her skirt to clear the spikes. There was rust and flakes of paint at the top of each spike. I saw one of them make a dent in the round flesh on the inside of her thigh. She stayed like that for a moment, with one leg on either side of the fence, looking down at me. A gust of wind made her hair cover her face. I could see the outline of each small tooth in her smiling mouth.

She could have been naked. She climbed down. When we reached the broken window she put her finger to her lips as if the need for silence had never been so strong. Standing under that window you couldn't have made a noise if you tried.

Inside you couldn't hear the noise of the diesel engines

any more. There was just the water, the mirrors and the porcelain. She waited for me to climb through the window and then she took my hand.

'You have to shut your eyes,' she said, as if it was going to be a surprise. I looked at her.

'Shut your eyes,' she said, 'shut them.'

From the light that came through my eyelids I guessed that she was taking me along the corridor where the lamps were like moths. There was a smell of fish organs, oil and scales. She was humming as she walked. The sound made me feel cold. She slowed down and the doors at the end of the corridor slapped open.

'Careful,' she said, when the doorframe brushed my shoulder. Her hand held mine softly. The light was harsher on the floor of the Plant. There was the smell of machinery and fish and another smell that you noticed on everyone in this town.

'You can open your eyes now,' she said, but I didn't open them immediately. First of all I thought about Sharon when she was asleep on the pile of nets. The shape she made with one palm open by her face, and her breathing like voices in an empty room.

I opened my eyes. I had never been so close to someone who was dead. You expect a corpse like that to look surprised, but Glennon didn't look surprised. You could tell that he had been dead for a while. Instead of the surface of his eye being glass-coloured it was crumpled like the wing of a fly.

The body was lying beneath the wooden slab where

Sharon worked. There was a pool of yellowish urine between its legs. You lie awkwardly when you're dead.

Sharon was looking at it as if it was a crack that had opened in the floor, but when her eyes reached the filleting knife in the ribs they started to open the way eyes, mouths, cunts open when they see something they recognize.

Glennon must have wondered why she had brought him there. His look as she approached him, that walk, silent on the balls of her feet, crushed hair, eyelids, breasts moving, the moist press, the knife held in fingertips that were drops of milky water.

We could have stayed there for ever with the wind banging on the factory roof. Three mouths fixed on what it's like to die. No black car, windows opening with a soft whine, or a perfect hand laying flowers.

Glennon must have been very still when the knife entered. Suddenly attentive, all eyes and ears. You could see that when you looked at the body. No detail would have been too small. But I didn't feel that way. Everything was distant. Not that anything had changed, but that I was standing a long way off, invisible, inaudible. But Sharon's mouth and eyes were open as if an invisible hand had gripped and twisted her skull, stretching the skin back from the eyes and forehead and forcing the jaw to open.

I hadn't heard the door open, but when I looked around I saw Albert Glennon standing between Sharon and me. His eyes were narrowed. His head swung to look at each of us, balanced on the point of each swing then dropped until he was looking at the body again. He stayed like that for a while, breathing heavily, a heartbeat in the jowl.

'What happened?' he asked. The voice was tiny in a pouch of fat that was pink and raw. No one answered.

'I warned him,' he said. He looked at Sharon for a long time, then he turned to me, lifting an eyebrow. I went over to Sharon.

'I have to go now.' She nodded. Her eyes were tired and black with the lethal cosmetics of the blood.

'One of ours,' he said, still looking at the body. When I left they were still standing there, neither moving nor touching.

Eighteen

There is a way of holding a petrol bomb when you throw it so that the petrol doesn't spill down your arm. You don't overfill it and you hold it the correct way.

Deeds taught me that. The time after they blew up the bus depot we spent an afternoon on the roof of the warehouse making petrol bombs. Deeds put sugar into the petrol so that it would stick like napalm, he said, and have the same sweet, oily smell. There was a warm breeze that day and you could almost smell the jungle's hot rain and insects.

He filled a whole crate with petrol bombs and hid them down at the Harbour. One of these days, he said, he was going to burn the whole town to the ground, walk along the street and destroy it the way he destroyed it in his mind every day with fountains of dust and fire following him, doorframes and plate glass bulging and splitting, loaves of bread, television sets, plastic bags and magazines spilling on to the street and people blown naked, tumbling limbs on the street, jackets, blouses and skirts flapping in useless breezes above the town.

While we were in the Plant Deeds had gone to the

Glennon house, following the tarmac drive as it made a crescent between two kerbs of granite whose grit of mica would soon be glittering in reflected light. He had gone to the front of the house. Maybe he walked on the lawn because the drive became gravel there and small stones might spatter to break the silence.

Maybe he stood there for a long time, suddenly attentive, rain on his glasses and the wire frames cold to the touch. Somewhere else in the town curtains are drawn and screens begin to flicker behind them with a blue light. Or someone is taking the film from the back of an Instamatic camera, waiting for the film to dry, gripping its sticky wetness between finger and thumb until it is as dry as it will ever be, and she looks at you from the photograph and her eyes say yes before you have a chance to black out the face until it is beyond help.

There is a way of holding a petrol bomb when you throw it so that the petrol doesn't spill down your arm. Deeds stood outside the Glennon house striking matches in the rain until the wick of the petrol bomb caught properly.

Deeds went up in flames on the lawn of the Glennon house, the petrol igniting with a soft sound like the wind in silk smooth as handled limbs, illuminating eyes hidden in haunted shadows, feathers on shoulderblades and bellies, the soft sounds they made to themselves.

When I came out of the Plant I saw the Scout sitting on the bonnet of Albert Glennon's car. The hand in the black leather glove rattled against the car and made the noise of all his dark walks, the sound of small cries under the trees of the Avenue at night, men with hungry faces and stripping fingers, women with sad, voracious eyes hanging skindeep, white sheets.

We saw the flames in the town, orange in the rain and low cloud. We stood there watching them. The cables holding the Polish ship creaked, lifting sheets of water as they tightened in the swell. I remembered what Deeds had said about putting the loft to his lips and blowing it towards the sea. You imagined the Polish boat slipping its moorings, climbing with lights.

When I looked away from the boat I saw the Scout grinning and twisting one hand against the other as if he was wringing a neck and I understood what had happened to the pigeons.

Nineteen

Every animal has a homing instinct, Deeds used to say. Some bright magnet in the flesh. That must have been the way I got from the Harbour to the path along the top of the Banks. I heard two sirens from the direction of the town. As soon as the sirens started there was movement and jolting noises from the cars parked in the Esplanade car park. I didn't realize what it was at first, and I remembered how Jammy wouldn't touch the coffins in the old graveyard because he said that sometimes they dug up a coffin and found long nailmarks on the inside of the lid. That meant that whoever was in the coffin wasn't really dead when they were buried. You woke up and it was completely dark and you couldn't move. Binty said that your nails and hair kept on growing after you were dead.

But when I heard the first engine start I knew what was happening. The noise I heard was of people climbing out of the back seats of the cars, zips being quickly fastened, skirts smoothed, damp panties being stuffed into handbags beside combs, lipstick, tissues and mirrors.

They would follow the ambulances as far as the Glennon house and the Plant and wait for them to load the bodies, one of which would be stiff and wettish and the other incandescent.

You imagined what the Esplanade would be like after that. Black with cars, their springs ticking.

'God, child,' Minnie said, when I looked into the toilets and saw her on the floor, 'you're soaked to the skin. I don't know why in the name of God you go around in the rain like that. You're not half-wise. Come in out of the rain like a good child.'

I sat down beside her and she handed me a bottle. I shivered when the wine touched my throat.

'Take her easy,' she said, pulling the bottle out of my hand. 'I'm starved for a bit of company these days with poor Binty gone. Not that he was the full shilling anyway. Then there was that poor friend of yours that fell off the roof. Break your heart so it would. If he was a child of your own you wouldn't feel any worse. Not that I've any worry on that score, and maybe I'm as well off.'

Down at the Harbour the yellow lights burned as if there were acres of barbed wire underneath and there was a smell of burning. If you looked closely you could see the blue lights of an ambulance.

'You think I don't know the stories they tell about me in this town. Mind you, I put lead in many a man's pencil but you wouldn't be up to the class of people you get in this town, the stories they come up with.'

She took a long drink from the bottle and put her hands to her stomach.

'Albert frigging Glennon,' she said slowly and I noticed for the first time that her voice was weak, 'he said he'd pay me to get rid of the child and not a red cent did I ever see. But he's paid me now.'

I realized that I hadn't seen her for days. I leaned forward and touched her. She was taut and her belly was as hard as a barrel of cement. She must have been sitting there since the day that Albert Glennon had come to her and started the memory of her baby ticking in her stomach like a fat clock. She started to groan as if she was going to spread her legs and have the ghost of a baby in front of my eyes.

Twenty

The day before Deeds' funeral I went down to the net store. The door was open and it moved in the wind. Under the building the incoming tide was beginning to cover the mud, its small fingers and thumbs surrounding the wooden pilings as if they were about to prise them out of the Harbour bottom.

The place was empty. Her clothes had gone. Even the shape of her body in the nets had disappeared. I waited. You always wait for something. Like when you stand at the back of a funeral and wait for the sound of heels on the gravel behind you, and the crowd between you and the grave opens with a moan. You don't look up but you know that the stranger's calves will whisper like silk as she walks and that she won't lift her veil and that her hands will be long and beautiful.

She had taken the debris out of the nets and left it on a shelf. I handled each piece. Starfish, sea-urchins, crab claws. I put them to my face and inhaled the way you do when you've spent the night with someone and the next day you put the tips of your fingers to your nostrils.

When I had done that I walked over to the hole in the

floor and sat down on the edge where I had seen her sit. The Polish freighter had left early the morning after we had been in the Plant and no one had seen Sharon since, so I wondered if the black water underneath me was beneath her feet and if she had stood on the deck and looked back at the town.

Then I saw something light-coloured in the mud at the edge of the water. It was hard to make out. It was one of the cups which had been standing on the table in the net store. I remembered the shape of her lips on the rim. I wondered if the black water was rising over her, cupping the hollow of her jaw, obliterating the blue shadow and filling her mouth.

Later I walked up the river to the warehouse. The door of the loft was open as well. Inside the door the wall was dark with rain and Deeds' magazine pictures tugged at the tacks which held them. You could see feathers trapped between the boards of the wall which moved in the draught. There were pigeon droppings on the floor.

I imagined the way it would have been on the night that the Scout killed the pigeons, the birds streaming in a circle around his head while he stroked them one by one from the air, wingbeats getting fainter against the frayed, black cuffs of his jacket. Before he laid them out in rows he must have folded the broken wings like gloves to cover the breasts and pink feet.

I walked on to the roof and looked downriver towards the Harbour. Behind me the door of the loft opened and closed in the wind the way doors in deserted towns open and close to remember their population.

The day of the funeral was still and cold. I stood at the back of the crowd. There was gravel under my feet. I could hear ropes slapping against the wood of the coffin. I looked behind me and saw Anne-Marie standing between the head-stones. She was wearing a black skirt and a white blouse under a black jacket. There was a veil pinned to her hair. All the women were wearing veils.

I stayed behind in the graveyard after the funeral. Two men strolled up with shovels, rolled up the artificial grass and started to fill in the grave. I heard earth strike the coffin and felt as if they were throwing everything in. Fish heads, old prams, grass clippings, builders' rubble, old bottles. Anything to make him stay down there. I left them to it and began to walk back towards the town.

Twenty-one

The next time I saw Minnie she was lying on her back in a hospital bed with her eyes closed. Her mouth was open. Every time her chest rose and fell there were half-breaths and whistles. The grey cuffs of her hair lay on the white pillow like ash. Her head didn't dent the pillow, as if she didn't weigh anything any more. The part of her eyelid that only shows when you are asleep was white and soft. Her belly supported the blankets and her knees were raised.

She was attached to a monitor by wires. Apart from her breathing the machine was the only other noise in the ward. I wondered what happened to the machine at night when there was no one else around. If it would sometimes show two heartbeats instead of one, the thick blue line I could see now and the bird's heartbeat of a child.

I stayed there for a long time but her eyes didn't open and the sound of her breathing didn't change. The light faded outside and no one came in to turn on the ward lights, so that it was as if her face was being covered with water and you could no longer see the blackheads and broken veins. The way Jammy was beautiful for a moment and then invisible.

Outside it didn't seem as dark. I turned at the gates of the hospital and looked back. Minnie was in one of the prefabs behind the main building. On my way down Mill Street I passed the gates of the Avenue. The trees stood out against the sky and they were bare like women's arms. I remembered Binty telling us the legend of the red woman when the fire at the Banks made bright tiles in Deeds' glasses, and when Binty got to the strangling part Deeds reached long fingers towards Jammy's throat and we all laughed.

The Submarine was ready to close when I got there. Chairs were stacked on tables. I cleared one table and sat down. No one came near me. The woman who owned the café came out to put the 'closed' sign on the door and dim the lights. She didn't look in my direction. She went back into the kitchen and I heard her talking about how Deeds had stabbed Glennon in the Plant and then had gone to the Glennon house with a petrol bomb. The way she talked, you knew she couldn't wait to get home and draw the curtains.

The frame of the pool room door held the darkness inside. At first I thought the breathless noises I could hear were voices from the pool room and for a moment I was aware of all the shadows around me. Then I looked up and saw Anne-Marie standing in front of me with a cup of tea in her hand and I knew that I had heard her walking between the tables, the blue and white checked nylon of her apron rustling.

She reached out to put the cup in front of me. I could

see moisture on her forearm and hand under the small hairs. The skin was white and the muscle on her arm was rounded. You imagined that it would be warm to touch, even though it looked bloodless. The cup shifted on the saucer as she put it down. She lifted another chair and sat down opposite me.

The tea grew cold. The owner left, shouting out in the darkness for Anne-Marie to lock up. We didn't speak. Her breathing was regular and deep as if she was asleep but her eyes were open and she seemed to be looking over my shoulder the way any woman looks over your shoulder when she is alone in the dark listening to the noise you make on top of her. We waited. As if we were all waiting, Sharon for her brief language, Deeds and Jammy for wings sifting the air and the soft sounds birds made to themselves, Binty for silk parachutes falling to earth and the click of heels across the beach.

Anne-Marie took my cup and saucer to the kitchen. When she came back she lifted both chairs on to the table. Outside she put her key in the lock and turned it. We walked down the Harbour road towards the Banks.

There were no formalities with her. You walked in silence until you found a spot and then you lay down. Once she got into her stride you knew that you might as well be anyone. It was almost as if you could get up and walk away and she would still be lying there, her eyes closed and her soft, little mouth probing the night air like the snout of some half-blind night creature.

We were on a patch of grass halfway down the cliff path.

If you looked up you could see the lights of the Harbour reflected on the underside of the low cloud, making the night seem twice as dark and full of flame.

Suddenly I remembered one of the pictures that Deeds had torn from a porn magazine and stuck to the wall of the loft. It showed a tomb in Paris. The man had been the founder of a fertility cult, Deeds told me, and the place was still a shrine. He was cast in bronze, lying on his back in a frock coat and top hat. The girl in the photograph wore a black veil. She had hitched up her black dress and straddled the lying figure, crushing her pink genitals against the bronze crotch.

I opened my eyes and saw that Anne-Marie's eyes were open and staring over my shoulder at the spot where I had talked with Deeds. I felt a chill run through me and forced her eyes to mine and kissed them and kissed them again, because as far as I was concerned there were no beautiful strangers and the only ghosts in this town are the ones that are walking the streets.

Love in History

One

Sergeant Gabriel Hooper had a Kodak monochrome photograph of Betty Grable on the wall of his room. In the photograph she was sitting astride the barrel of an anti-aircraft gun. Her skin was white and her lips were drawn back from her teeth in a smile that captured the light of an entire aircraft carrier.

If you pulled down the top of Betty Grable's swimming costume, the breasts underneath would be white shaved cones with exact, graphite tips.

In 1944 the uniform crotches of USAF pilots were stiff with beauty.

Sergeant Gabriel Hooper had been stationed at RAF Cranfield since 1942. His billet was in a Nissen hut beside the seven salty miles of runway. Sand blown up from the beach piled against the seaward gable wall. New hangars creaked in derelict breezes and the red singing tongue of a windsock pointed towards Russian winters and Tripoli landings.

At night he sat on his bed in USAF shorts and singlet writing letters to his wife in handwriting that seemed like some complicated calculation of crosswinds and velocity over target. Somewhere in Kansas or Oklahoma was a dusty mailbox crammed with letters that his wife never answered.

He kept a photograph of himself and his wife in his breast pocket. The pocket of a dead pilot is often found to contain a rabbit's foot or photobooth snapshot from a port entrance or railway station or other point of departure.

Hooper shared the billet with Sergeant Hardy. Hardy smoked cigars and dealt five-stud one-handed in a poker game that ran from the spring of 1942 to the summer of 1945 in the back room of the lighthouse café, a game that raged through El Alamein and the siege of Stalingrad and the night the squadron burned Berlin, when less than half of the planes returned and the sky over the burning Potsdamerplatz was full of IOUs signed in Hardy's fugitive hand.

There were two beds and two lockers and a suitcase under Hardy's bed that was full of Wild Turkey, Lucky Strikes and a baseball glove with Hardy's name in red stitching on the wrist. At the window there was a brass telescope on a tripod, which Hardy had won from a Kentucky rear gunner. Hooper explained to Hardy how light refracts through a system of convex mirrors facilitating the study of the orbs.

Hardy would turn out the light in the room and sit in the dark to improve his night vision. Then, whistling through his teeth, he would use the telescope to identify waitresses behind the curtains of the canteen changing room by the shape of their orbs and the outline of their convexities.

If Hooper used the telescope he looked for Betelgeuse and Sirius, the dog star. He looked for the coast of America, the smell of pancakes, the taste of beech nut passed from one mouth to another in the front seat of a pick-up parked behind a half-empty grain silo.

In the bedroom of 1944 Adelene fastened the catch of her brassière around her waist and twisted its stiff points upwards and around to put it into place. With a sweater over the top her breasts were like the tops of pencils, her black hair was a replica in lacquer and her white thighs stormed the territory of the heart.

During the day Adelene counted Cellophane packets of American stockings and ate American peaches from the tin with her fingers. At night pilots held her against the perimeter fence, flattening her breasts against their tunic pockets. When she took a job in the aerodrome canteen she adjusted her lipstick using the polished tea-urn as a mirror in which pilots returning from missions looked for her mouth, lurid with desire or grief.

She rolled the American brown stockings up her legs and put on the black patent shoes with the Cuban heel. From her bedroom you could hear bombers practising night landings at the aerodrome. She looked into the mirror with the brown tip of a hairpin between her lips and thought about an incendiary sky over Dresden, terrible with white pearls of men's flesh.

Adelene boarded with Mrs Nelligan. Mrs Nelligan spent

her evenings drinking alone in the parlour. She lifted the baby from the pram and took a bottle of gin out of the well of the pram. There were rings in the polish of the table where glasses had been set. There were marks on the wood-work where cigarettes burned blindly through the darkness of Mrs Nelligan's oblivion.

On her first night in the house Adelene heard the baby crying. She crept downstairs to find Mrs Nelligan in a stained camisole, laddered tights and in tears. As Adelene helped her to bed she gripped the front of Adelene's dressing gown. 'Were you ever', she said, 'crossed in love?'

Every night, before she went out, Sadie Poland knocked on Adelene's door and came in without waiting for an answer. She had blond hair and a roll of fat around her waist like a moneybelt. She would lie on Adelene's bed and spill flecks of Adelene's nail polish on to the bedspread and ask Adelene questions.

'Are you for the Vogue tonight, pet?'

'I'm working.'

'The Melody Aces are playing.'

'The Melody Aces. Fancy.'

'One of the pilots asked me. He's a ride so he is. He's a mad thing. I near ate the lipstick off myself when I seen him coming at me. It's different with a Yank.'

Sadie lifted a blouse from the back of a chair and held it against her.

'God, Adelene, I'd give a pension for a figure like yours.'

'Is Ma Nelligan on the drink again?'

'Out of the mind.'

Adelene unscrewed a fingertip of lipstick from its gold cylinder and pursed her lips. She's the letter from home and the telegram on the hall table. She's Miss USAF of 1942 and 1943 and 1944 and all the lonely months scattered like personal effects.

They heard movement from the next room along the corridor. Sadie turned her eyes up.

'There's your man now,' she whispered and giggled.

'I know the type of that Morris,' Adelene said, 'the way he licks them lips when he looks at you, it'd make you sick. Your skin crawls at the thought.'

'What you need's a big Yank,' Sadie said. What you need is a big mad thing to take you out of the Vogue ballroom and eat the face off you and the next day he'd be gone to England or America or baled-out at 10,000 feet with the light of Europe burning under his bootsoles and his mouth bitter without your kiss.

'The man on the wireless said it's going to snow,' Adelene said quietly. That snow was already falling on the Atlantic. Snow unmelted on grey northern waters and U-boats lonely in the polar darkness underneath. It made you cold to think of it.

Two

The Reverend William Morris lay on his bed in the next room listening to the sound of women's voices, his thin petrol-coloured lips set and his eyes closed. The jacket of his black suit and a bag of tracts lay on the chair beside the bed. Six months ago the Reverend Morris had stepped off the Belfast train. As soon as he had stepped from the carriage he had recognized it as a town of adulterers and fornicators and intoxicators, where the women wore their skirts up around their arses and went with men how many times a night without shame, so that the very foot he set on the ground seemed scorched with the knowledge.

Morris was born in the pound beside the Harland and Wolfe shipyard in Belfast. In the year of his birth the unfinished hull of the *Titanic* climbed above the wall, towards a dream of empty yellow lifejackets floating among broken packing cases. At the end of his street women from the shirt factory got off trams and walked down the pavement towards their homes. His mother watched them.

'Papish bitches,' she said, 'you'd think they owned the place.'

Men threw rivets at them from the scaffolding around

the *Titanic*. He saw a woman blinded. In January 1930 he preached his first mission in the Shankhill Road gospel hall. The shoes of the congregation carried unmelted snow across the wooden floor. His voice was the wind in the corrugated tin walls. The congregation were roused and got to their feet and the wooden folding chairs shifted and howled like the souls of the damned.

He remembers the shipyard workers putting down their tools to listen to Carson. He remembers his mother and the other women kneeling in their back entrance banging tin binlids against the ground. He remembers the honey wagon coming down the hill from the abattoir the way it did every evening, and the children going one two buckle my shoe, and the man who sold fish.

In 1938 his mother died in the back bedroom. He heard her call his name and went into the bedroom where she was sitting on the commode. 'Listen,' she said, grabbing the sleeve of his coat. He couldn't hear anything. 'The Pope of Rome's coming,' she said, and when he said 'The Pope's not coming here, Ma,' she said, 'Can you not hear his cohorts?' and collapsed on to the commode, her bowels rustling as if a bird was trapped under her thighs. The thick sherbet smell of death filled the air around his head so that he remembered spikenard and saffron, calamus and cinnamon with all trees of frankincense, myrrh and aloes with all the chief spices.

That was when he was really alone. That was when his mother's clothes would dream limbs to wear them and pursue him through the corridors of his mind. He preached in the cornmarket, believing that his voice could break windows.

He preached to the prostitutes on Amelia Street. Their voices whispered in his ear like human smoke.

Whores of Rome, he said later, they tempted him to drink, and he was consumed with a thirst that raged in the ledges of his skull and would not be slaked. He awoke one night in a cheap room to see four pathfinder flares in each corner of the sky over the shipyards lighting up the cranes in the docks and the slate roofs of the shipyard workers' houses and outlining the shape of a woman in the bed beside him.

By the time he got to the shipyard there was nothing left of the street except a thick lens of melted window glass on the pavement.

The Reverend William Morris lay on his bed listening to the voices of women in the room next door and to their feet crossing the landing. He went to the door and pressed his eye to the keyhole, where he could see their stocking legs on the boards. Stockings that weren't given to them for nothing. Skirts that fell in folds on his heart. The crotch of the preacher's trousers sagged with the weight of forty years of longing.

It is the winter of 1944. The preacher places the bony yellow palms of his hands against his temples and puts his fingers in his ears so that he cannot hear their voices. The devil is the chance of love neglected or denied. He kneels

on the linoleum feeling through his trousers the blue heads
of carpet tacks and tries to pray, but he can't and is alone
with his eyes and his hands and his dirty, dirty mind.

Three

Each Saturday night a truck left the airfield for the town.
The truck brought aircrews to the Aurora cinema or the
Vogue ballroom. Gabriel Hooper sat under the canvas flaps
beside the tailgate where he could see bombers practising
night landings at the runway, the red flares of their exhausts
like islands burning in a smoky archipelago across the
Pacific.

When the truck pulled up outside the Aurora the street
was busy with men in uniform, their pockets full of Fanny
Maes toffees, razor blades and silk stockings. They were
watched ravenously from windows and mirrors by thousands of women with red lips and starved fox fur collars.
Hardy jumped over the tailgate of the moving truck.

'See you later,' he said, tapping Hooper on the foot.

Hooper got off a minute later and crossed the street to
the Aurora where there was a full-length poster of Betty
Grable beside the glass box office. He checked his watch.
He was early. The box office was empty. Hooper lit a
cigarette and began to walk towards the square. Others
were moving towards the square. Soldiers, pilots, men with
forged petrol coupons to sell or exchange, prostitutes who

travelled down on the train every Saturday night and returned the next morning carrying money, watches, keepsakes and stories of wives who desert, like a dress slipping from a whore's body in another country. Sometimes they bring tears back because it is the winter of 1944 and it's all right to bunch a woman up like a pillow and soak her with tears. Sometimes there are bruises as well.

Hooper had heard preachers like this one before at railhead cattle sales or fairs. Anywhere that there was a crowd there was the possibility of redemption. Morris was standing on a small wooden box in the middle of the square. The sound of his voice had drawn ground crews from Alabama and the Mississippi delta. Hooper joined the crowd, pressed up against a black man in fitter's overalls whose lips moved as he listened.

'Where', Morris asked, 'will you spend eternity?' He promised that sinners would burn in hell for ever, that the smell of roasting flesh was present in his thin nostrils, that every tongue would confess the name of Jesus. Beside Hooper the fitter clapped his hands softly together as he moved. The palms were pink, like unhealed burns.

Or the inside of a woman's lips. The fitter swayed against Hooper as he had swayed in gospel halls and wooden barns and as the tone of the preaching changed he sighed at the thought of remembered concupiscence on a preacher's tongue in the soundless heat of a delta night.

'Friends, I call upon you to bear witness to the abominations of the Church of Rome. Me and you know the methods of Rome. Its handmaidens surround us on every side. Their tongues are honey. Their garments are of the finest silk and lace and we are made drunk, Revelations 17:2, with the wine of their fornication.'

'That sure is some preacher,' the fitter said, when Morris had finished. He took a cigarette from behind his ear.

'Best I ever heard.'

Hooper looked up the street. There was a queue outside the Aurora. Already couples were leaving the Vogue and crossing the square towards the towpath that led past Hagan's mill and the empty coal basin where spilled grain gleamed like prairie dawn on the black water. There was a smell of bonemeal from the mill that was like the smell in the boots and armpits of aircrews waiting for dawn. Darling. It's different with a Yank.

'Heard it's going to snow,' the fitter said, stamping his feet, 'colder than a witch's tit in this square anyhow.' When Hooper didn't answer him the fitter spat and turned away.

'Preacher got you shook anyway,' he said.

Hooper joined the queue outside the Aurora and followed it into the heat. He sat at the front of the balcony, close to the cast-iron heater. Tip-up seats rattled in the stalls in front of him. As the house lights went down someone put their knees against the back of his seat and a girl laughed.

When the newsreel began Hooper scanned the faces of men alighting from ships, the face of a man with sunburn drinking from a tin mug, a man lying on the edge of a trench with his arm thrown over the barrel of a gun and his lips drawn back from his teeth in a smile of recognition at the shadow that has followed him from a street with a foundry at one end and a gasworks or a tannery at the other.

'Most cheerful fucking corpse I ever seen,' someone said behind Hooper.

There was footage of a dead horse buried up to its nostrils in snow with its hooves in the air and a burnt-out church in the background. Then there were Russian women in headscarves polishing brass shells or filling sandbags.

'Them Olgas,' another voice said and the row behind Hooper laughed. But Hooper scanned the faces as if he would find one he knew, or recognize familiar hands arid with dry flour or cement dust.

Because this is the war you fought in and these are the lethal signs of home and them Olgas won't leave you alone. You want their eyes and their hands and the chapped skin on their elbows and heels. You want to ride their dreams, their large families in one-bedroom flats, their Molotov cocktails, cheap underwear, tired eyes, dirty sheets.

As the titles of the film came up the sound of aeroplane engines rattled the glass of the box office, circling over the town until the last plane had settled into formation during the first reel, a sound to dislodge a kiss from Betty Grable's faithless lips and shake the compass of a navigator's uncertain heart.

Sadie heard the planes as well, waiting in the alley behind the Vogue, and she looked up. It was a narrow, concrete alley with crates of Cantrell and Cochrane lemonade bottles piled on either side. It smelt of cinema toilets and of the damp corridors of air between clouds. Above her head the lead plane broke off, drawing the squadron after it towards the radio beacon at Bishopscourt forty miles away. In less than two hours' time the squadron would cross the coast of Holland, with the fires of Rotterdam to the north and the fires of Bremerhaven to the south like a procession of torches across Europe.

Four

Sadie met him in the Vogue. She looked up and he was standing in front of her, dressed to desolation in his sergeant's uniform. He asked her to dance and they moved on to the dance-floor. He could, she thought, dance on a saucer and was good-looking enough to take the light out of your eye. Afterwards they sat on the balcony. He came from Butte, Montana. He told her about the sheep drovers who came down out of the mountains ten days' walk away with red dust on their boots and their tongues hanging out.

He told her the mountains do funny things to a man. He told her how nearly everybody in the town stayed indoors when the drovers came down out of the high pasture at night, their eyes wild with loneliness.

'Are you a drover?' she asked.

'No. My folks got a boarding house in the town.'

'Fancy,' she said. Fancy a wooden house with wooden steps up to it and a sign saying 'Rooms' above the door. Fancy men spending all that time alone with sheep and wolves at the edge of the trees. The band began to play 'Strangers in the Night'. The drummer had his jacket off and in the dark the two patches of sweat under his arms looked like the eyes, you would swear, of a man wild with loneliness.

They left the ballroom together. Sweat drying between her girdle and skin pricked the flesh on her shoulders and hips. America, she thought, what cars they have there. Lincoln, Dodge sedan. She ran her hand along the bonnets of cars parked on the street. I'd like a Sunbeam, she thought, or a Humber, dreaming. She saw another airman watching her from across the street and she danced a few steps so that the gravel scattered from under her shoes like planets.

'What is it like,' she said, 'to run a boarding house?'

What is it like to run a boarding house in Butte, Montana? What is it like when you kiss a man with a moustache? What is it like when you kiss a man with a moustache in the back seat of a Dodge sedan when the night wind kisses the window and the tumbleweed brushes the chrome bumper like the moustaches of America, his fingers twisted in your nightweed like white, broken things?

Before he could answer there was the sound of a truck horn from the square.

'I got to go,' he said. He cupped her chin in his hand and tilted her mouth. He was wearing a gold ring on the little finger of his left hand and there were small hairs trapped behind the ring. His lips tasted of spearmint.

'Maybe next week?' he said.

All that week she told Adelene how her and Bud were

going to open a boarding house in Butte, Montana. That Bud couldn't stand a woman with drink on her breath. Said there was nothing worse than a woman with drink on her breath except maybe a woman fighting and that he hated it when someone was late. How she had asked him if there was any work in Butte, Montana, and he had laughed and said honey, where I come from there's only one way for a girl to make money – and what, she wondered, did he mean by that?

She looked at her watch again. It was cold in the alley behind the Vogue. She thought about standing at a window in America where there was only silence, the warm silence of dust and lizards on the highway.

Bud put his arms around her from behind.

'I never seen you coming,' she said, 'you near put the wits out of me.'

'Didn't meant to scare you, honey.'

'I got palpitations now.'

'You never told me your name,' he said.

'That's for me to know and you to find out.' She turned until she was facing him. His moustache brushed her forehead.

'It'd freeze you out here,' she said, 'is it cold where you come from?'

'Snow in the winter and hotter than the hob of hell in the summer.'

'The way you talk,' she said.

The front of his uniform smelt of starch. The tip of his moustache brushed her forehead and he kissed her. After a minute she pushed him away.

'Take it easy, don't eat the mouth off me.' She was standing with her back against the crates of lemonade bottles.

'You're hurting me. Oh God, mind the stockings.'

'I'll give you more,' he said. His hands were twisted in her clothes. She could taste blood in her lips, the mouth cut off her as if it might never heal. She tried to pull away from him and the crates behind her toppled on to the ground, and she fell back among the bottles and crates hearing her stockings ladder, but there would be another pair, and another, while the war lasted and the planes went overhead, and you stood at your bedroom window on a warm night and imagined you could see the light of fires in Europe. She saw the drovers coming down out of the high pastures at night, the weight of their loneliness cracking the mountains and boulders of Butte, Montana, under their heels.

She felt numb from the waist down, as if pinned beneath a beam in a falling house, as she had seen so often in newsreels. Suspicious of gas leaks and water rising in the cellar, pinned under the darkness of rubble she had often imagined in her bed at night, with a siren sounding the all-clear across the aerodrome, the town, the cities of Europe and the wide spaces of America where women lay with their legs in the air like white flags in the mountains and high sheep pastures of Butte, Montana.

She understood that he would climb out of the bottles and brush off the front of his uniform, place stockings or Babe Ruth chocolate or tinned fruit on one of the crates and wait for her to fix her skirt. Over his shoulder she could see the white of her knee showing through the laddered stocking and wondered if she could fix it, as Adelene did, with a single drop of nail varnish that hardened like solder, fixing a hole after each Saturday night so that the stocking glittered on her legs with beads of nail polish like the toxic jewels of deceit.

In the last reel Hooper watched Betty Grable's hydraulic smile unfold her lips on perfect teeth. Cigarette smoke rose from the stalls. Woodbines, Sweet Afton. The smell of hot film from the projection room drifted across the balcony and the mute upturned faces of the audience and Betty Grable bared enough leg to take a navigator's breath away.

The house lights came up with the credits and there was a sound from the back row of the balcony like stretched nylon. Hooper followed the audience out into the foyer. There was a girl standing beside the poster of Betty Grable. She took a compact from a clutch bag and studied her face. She moved her head from side to side then smoothed an eyebrow with a wetted fingertip.

Her hair was a replica in lacquer. She saw him looking and smiled and closed the compact with a snap and moved so that she was standing in the same pose as Betty Grable in the poster behind her, holding it long enough for Hooper to look from one to the other and decide that they might be sisters, the girl's smile directed now at the poster saying my lips are as full as yours, and my legs as long and my breasts are creamy, O my sister.

Before Hooper could move or speak she was gone. Hooper remembered that his wife had not accompanied him to the station when he had left home. He remembered taking the bus from the top of the road to the railhead and watching while he waited for her to appear at the door of the house. Later, sitting on the train as it pulled out of the small station somewhere in Kansas or Oklahoma, he had shut his eyes to evoke the departure he had hoped for. The hiss of brakes and the last, desperate impress of a woman's lips against the carriage glass streaked with condensation and dirt.

He pushed through the crowd at the door and reached the street, knowing before he got there that the girl would have disappeared into the knot of couples in front of the Vogue and the Aurora.

Five

Hooper flew deliveries of combat aircraft across the Irish Sea and into Europe, his eyes fixed on small fields, dykes, canals and cypress trees. They are the landscape of the lost heart. When snow grounded all flights he sat on his bed drawing diagrams to describe the thermals that would lift you over the mountains towards the Atlantic.

The next morning he saw snow on the wire of the perimeter fence. Beyond that a line of men with brooms moved down the main runway. Looking out of the window he saw Hardy being towed down the runway behind a jeep on the blade of a square shovel. Hardy looked up and waved one hand as the snow spurted out from under the shovel.

His wife had never seen snow. He had first met her in a diner near his home. He had come into town to get some fencing wire. The wire sat in bales on the back of his truck outside the diner where he had come for coffee. The loudest sound in America was the sound of his cup on the stainless steel counter when he saw her come in through the door, and when she spoke it seemed as if her voice was the sound of a train crossing the skyline from east to west.

Now it seemed as if he could no longer remember the

sound of a train, or of her voice or how he had followed her out of the diner and spoken to her. Silence surrounded her name.

He had sat behind her in church counting the tiny pearls in her white fascinator hairnet. He had sat with her in the lobby of the bank watching her hands fasten and unfasten the clasp of the white patent handbag she had held in the crook of her elbow all through their marriage ceremony and at church in the years after that, until the day when she wrapped it in tissue and put it in the back of the wardrobe and looked at him as if he was something she'd never seen before like snow.

They had talked about the price of grain. He would stand outside in the evening and look at the sky as if he would see the price of grain written there like the floating dust on the still water of a farmyard cistern. At night he sat on the edge of the bed looking at the stiff, fair hairs on her arms and her lip while she slept.

'In winter,' she said, 'it snows every day in Chicago.' And there's a wind that blows down the avenues and deposits snow in the unswept entrances of alleyways and dry hearts. Hooper looked at the yellow clouds on the skyline beyond the aerodrome. He took the photograph from his wallet and thought of her in the ruins of a city, behind wire, or sitting with other women in the back of a truck that will drive for miles until it reaches a wood or a river. He sees her in Paris, kissing Americans, with her back against a tree in the rue Lafayette holding the hem of her skirt in one hand and gripping a fistful of khaki uniform with the other and wondered whether he should write to her of snow.

He could not remember the freckles on her face or the light, sour touch of a wife's lips like sweat drying between the shoulderblades.

Hardy came in with snow on the lapels of his tunic. He went to the window and shifted a matchstick from one corner of his mouth to the other.

'That new girl in the canteen,' he said, 'talk about tits.'

The day Hooper's call-up papers arrived he walked into the kitchen where she was sitting at the table with the opened envelope in front of her. He took it out of her hands and read the letter. Without a word she began to lift things from the kitchen shelves and throw them on to the floor. She threw down all the pans and the jars of preserves. She emptied the floor bin on to the ground at his feet and swept the kettle off the top of the stove. Hooper sat down. There was flour mixed with dust on his boots. Finally she lifted the big wooden calendar that had been a wedding present and threw it so that it hit the doorframe and split open and all the dates and years fell on to the floor and she sat down beside him, holding her hands over her ears as if she could hear the terrible sound of all her days spilling on to the wooden boards: that day, that year and the year before, the thirties and the New Deal and all the years before that and all the years to come stretching before them across thousands of acres of grasslands and dirt roads and whirlwinds that cross the dustbowl bearing with them the faces of the known dead.

'Lord, Hooper,' Hardy said, 'some of them girls is as easy as spit.'

He pulled a wooden chair towards him with the toe of his boot and sat backwards on it, facing Hooper with his arms folded on the back.

'You know your problem, Hooper. You don't know how to enjoy yourself. Take my word for it. I seen guys like you before. Just keep getting miserabler and miserabler and there ain't no cure except getting their ass shot off. Take my word for it and get a woman. Some of them'll drop them for you quick as you can say Washington DC.'

Or the names of the remote alleys of remembrance Hooper inhabited in German airspace at night when the expectation of death overpowered the sound of a wife's kiss and the name of a town in Kansas or Oklahoma.

'A good screw'll sort it out,' Hardy said softly, 'take my word. Any post?'

Hooper shook his head. There was the sound of aeroplane engines from the far end of the runway. Adelene crossed in front of the window on a bicycle.

'Tits,' Hardy said, 'and legs that go right on up, you know what I mean.' He watched her cycle towards the gate.

'There's a Betty Grable on at the Aurora tonight,' he said, 'you coming?'

'I might.'

'You sure like that Betty Grable, Hooper. I never seen a man that liked her the way you do.'

It's the way the wind rattles the tin roof at night when you lie awake and alone that makes you imagine the drumming of Betty Grable's immaculate heels.

Hardy reached under the bed for the handle of the suitcase, and pulled it towards him and opened it. He removed cigarettes and two packets of stockings. He winked at Hooper.

'You never can tell,' he said. Hooper turned on to his stomach and looked again at the photograph. He was sitting on a deckchair. Behind him was a water-tower and beyond that the grass stretched towards a monotone skyline. His wife sat between his legs, looking into the sun, expressionless as a woman of Europe, deprived of time and place to mourn.

Six

The airfield was near capacity. There were almost four hundred aircraft in storage at the base. Ground crew dismantled weapons and removed munitions for storage in the ordnance sheds. A groupage unit was established in a Nissen hut behind hangar sixteen to chart the location of each aircraft. There was more than one knife fight outside the Vogue.

A radio operator from Michigan shot himself with a revolver in the shower block. There was soap in his hair and his clothes were on a peg beside the shower stall. In his pocket they found an unaddressed letter, a cinema ticket and an earring-back.

Adelene and the other girls gathered at the window of the canteen to watch General George Patton review the troops. Patton stood on a wooden platform in the middle of the main runway. B-24s and B-17s were drawn up in front of him. Ground crew and pilots stood in ranks between the planes. When the general moved his head the celluloid peak of his cap flickered like metal. Afterwards he was driven to the officers' mess in a jeep, passing the window of the canteen so that they saw him clearly in the front of the jeep, smoking a cigar and wearing dark glasses from *Life* magazine.

Adelene watched him carefully as he passed. She was curious about what generals thought about. She wondered if the dark glasses were a sign of some private unease that he carried with him. Perhaps when he should have been thinking about armies or new fronts on the Rhine, some part of his mind could still hear the dark, elusive voice of Tokyo Rose, the subversion of her voice carried in the air across the Pacific and washed up on endless West Coast beaches.

The canteen was a green Nissen hut between the main hangars and the spare parts dump. It was open day and night. Pilots came in at dawn, still wearing their parachutes and flying jackets. Their eyes were glazed with altitude, stunned at reflections of mortality in a tiny window above the earth. They drank black coffee before dawn briefings, gave Adelene letters to post and fell in their thousands through unfamiliar clouds.

On the wall of the canteen there was a photograph of Captain Nonsense. The Operations Record book recalled that a B-24 piloted by Captain Nonsense landed from Langford Lodge at 1245 hrs on 14 May 1943. He stayed until 1355 hrs, time enough for a coffee in the canteen and for his photograph to be taken in front of his aircraft, the Suzy Q decal partly obscured by his head. He would carry in his palm like loose change the imperceptible scrape of the blonde canteen girl's fingernails right up until the August of that year, when he was shot down along with others at Foggia during the Ploesti raid.

In September a Lockheed Ventura emerged from fog and landed on an uncompleted ancillary runway. Convinced that he had landed in Belgium, Captain Van der Los held members of the forty-second depot repair squadron at bay with a revolver while the aircraft sank into the runway and the cement dried around its wheels until it seemed that it would be fixed there, stalled in a denial of flight. Afterwards Van der Los bought them all a drink in the bar of the Lighthouse café and later that night joined Hardy's poker game in the back room.

The Lighthouse café stood at the seaward end of the runway overlooking the lighthouse in the estuary beyond. Its cement walls were streaked with damp and its roof was patched where the unretracted undercarriage of a P-38 Mustang had removed a yard of slates on take-off. Before Van der Los's arrival the mud flats and bends of the estuary were full of birds. They built nests on the concrete pontoons that supported the landing lights and filled the air at night with small cries like the lost objects on the rim of a radar screen.

Until Van der Los, crazed by nights of bourbon, blackjack and Cape memories that littered the edges of his mind like carrion took to standing up to his neck in the estuary mud with a loaded .22 rifle and the acrid taste of spare brass cartridges in his mouth.

'Them fucking birds man,' he said, 'they stop your sleep, I tell you.'

Seven

The snow thawed and it was a wet spring. In newspapers and magazines red flags inched across the map of Europe, and Betty Grable's blacknailed fingertip inched across the map of the heart.

Hooper was transferred to tuition. They arrived from Kansas and Oklahoma and South Dakota for gunnery practice on the beach and the mournful thermals and radio fixes of Sergeant Hooper's navigation class. They pressed girls against the perimeter fence and dreamed of being trapped in harness with the ground approaching at ten frames per second, mid-air collisions, undercarriage shot to pieces, being found floating in the sea with the wet silk of a parachute trailing behind them and their voices choked by oil and debris and longing.

Adelene stood at the window. A suspender buckle lay cold and blue against the inside of her thigh. She could hear the baby crying downstairs, and Mrs Nelligan moving the dial of the wireless incessantly between stations. There was a glow of landing lights over the aerodrome. A low loader came slowly up the road carrying a plane. Both wings were broken off and the cockpit glass was starred. There was a soldier standing on the trailer with a long pole in his hand. Every time they came to a place where the telegraph wires crossed the road he used the pole to lift the wire over the wrecked plane. The trailer drew level with Adelene's window so that she was looking directly into the soldier's face. She leaned forward until her forehead touched the glass and the material of her slip stuck to the condensation on the window. The soldier stared at her for a minute then turned until he was facing front again. Adelene watched him as the truck moved off, his back rigid with the consequences of departure.

She had been standing at the window the night Sadie came home from her meeting with Bud and walked into the house and locked the door of her room against expectation then lay on her bed and wept. She wept for herself. She wept for America and its impossible silences. Then she got up and opened the wardrobe. She stood in front of it for a long time, then she removed all her clothes from it and carried them carefully downstairs and out into the back garden. When she had finished with the clothes she took the shoeboxes from the bottom of the wardrobe, carrying them downstairs unopened in her outstretched arms as if each contained footsteps in the dust of her future nights.

She found a bottle of pink paraffin in the scullery and Adelene had watched as she scattered it over the pile of clothes, then struck a match over the blouses, skirts and coats, the slingbacks, the crocodile skins, and the black patents with a stiletto so high you thought you were Lana Turner. She had remained outlined against the fire for a long time like a survivor who stood in a street bombed to the horizon, stunned and unable to believe either that they had survived or that they had lost everything.

Just before dawn she had walked into Adelene's room without knocking and shaken Adelene awake.

'Would you lend us your black skirt,' she had said, 'I'm meeting Bud tonight and I haven't a stitch to wear.'

Adelene turned and went back to the dressing table. She lapped Pond's cold cream on to a knob of cotton wool and passed it over her face. She licked the tip of an eyebrow pencil and began to draw in her eyebrows with a navigator's precision, with allowance for drift, for winds and weather from across the Atlantic. She added lipstick and kissed the excess on to pieces of tissue.

She stayed in front of the mirror for a long time. On these Saturday nights in the hinterland of war you're the gleam in the projectionist's eye. They take you out along the perimeter fence or down the towpath and ask your name, and the name they want to hear is already on their lips. They show you photographs of women as if they were someone you would recognize. And all the time scared out of their wits of the letter that says Dear John, I have gone. Your love isn't worth a click of the fingers to me no more, you was glad to go to the war. They take you down alleyways and hurt you with their fear.

Adelene put on her coat and went out into the hallway. She knocked once on Sadie's door but there was no answer. Downstairs she listened for a minute at the door of the sitting room because sometimes Sadie talked to Mrs Nelligan, but all she could hear was wireless static through which a foreign voice faded in and out like a mayday from some skirmish long since over. She closed the hall door softly behind her.

After they got out of the truck Van der Los took a flask out of his pocket and handed it to Hardy. Hardy folded his forage cap under his epaulette and gulped at the flask.

'You believe that guy Hooper?' he said.

'Seen it happen sometimes.'

'Guy lies on his bed for three years, then all of a sudden he's like Clark Gable. I wouldn't of believed it. Hair slicked back and all. Going to the movie? I says. Ballroom, he says. Like that.'

'See it happen,' Van der Los said, 'man makes up his mind.'

They walked up the street and joined the queue outside the Vogue. A girl squealed with laughter outside the Satellite café and ran a small distance. Van der Los watched her. His eyes were the colour of the sky above the clouds seen through filmed Perspex when the knowledge of sub-zero temperatures made you freeze up inside your flying suit.

'Man gets hungry for a woman,' he said, 'you feel it in your belly.'

They moved aside when two military policemen came down the steps of the Vogue dragging a young soldier between them. There were batons in their free hands. The soldier's hair was damp and matted with blood. His mouth was a red rose.

'See the little girl tonight?' Van der Los asked.

'No. No more of that warm pussy,' Hardy said, laughing.

Further down the street other men were standing at the bar of Rice's Select Lounge, drinking beer and watered Four Roses bourbon that the owner bought from Hardy. They leaned on the counter with their caps pushed back on their heads and their tunics unbuttoned watching for a woman, the beginnings of a fight or deliverance from the fear that finds you at 20,000 feet in the smell of warm oil and your own piss. They avoided Hooper, who finished his drink at the bar and left without ordering another.

Eight

Morris crossed the hallway in his stockinged feet and tried and then opened Adelene's door. It was the first time he had been alone in a woman's room since he had sat on the bed in his parents' room in Prussia Street sucking sherbet from a liquorice stick and looking out through the window at the derricks in the shipyard and the masts of a ship in the drydock that flew a blue flag that Lukie Maginn said was the flag of Peru.

The curtains were drawn. He could smell the unmade bed, the workclothes stained with spilled tea, wiped cutlery and perspiration on the back of a chair, the unspecified contents of drawers and the darkness that the room offered like a black gag bitter with scent. He went to the dressing table and fingered its bottles: Pond's, Max Factor. He dipped his finger into an open box of talcum powder and touched his mouth. The taste was bitter like copper. He remembered the black liquorice stick and the dissolution of sherbet under the tongue.

There was a stocking hanging over the mirror. He took it down and ran the back of his hands along it, snagging it on the quick of his thumbnail. He took off his jacket and rolled his shirtsleeve to the shoulder then drew the stocking up his arm and stared into the mirror, the stocking on his arm like a glove of her absence.

Inside the ballroom Hooper watched Adelene dance in arms that smelt of Palmolive. He watched her with such intensity that his eyes could have pierced immeasurable distances of war and desolation to reach the exact spot under the left breast where Betty Grable's monochrome heart pumped Pearl Harbor or Omaha Beach through paper veins. He drew a Lucky Strike from the paper packet and tapped unanswerable signals with the tip of the cigarette on the lid of the packet.

She watched him approach in the mirrored lid of a powder compact. When he asked her to dance she answered 'yes', and he smiled the wide, blue smile of a drought in the cornbelt.

'I never seen you before,' she said close to his ear. I never noticed you in the canteen. I never seen you drunk like the others. I never seen you playing baseball behind the hangars, or dancing like a flag in white USAF shorts with the other men when they swim on the beach, standing waistdeep in the water or floating on their backs smoking like *Daily Mail* photographs of endless husbands floating in the shallow, oily waters of Dunkirk.

'I've seen you before,' he said. I've seen your red lips in the canteen after a late shift as I lay awake and alone. I've heard you laugh with men as I lay alone when the sound of a wife's kiss is the sound of Betty Grable's heart broken with frost in the night.

'Fancy a drink?' she said. 'I'm parched.' They went to the balcony. He fetched two cups of tea. 'Do you miss home?' she asked. 'Are you homesick?'

How many in your family? Are you married? He held out the photographs of his wife and himself mutely, as if they were the victims of an accident, without mentioning dates of birth, or the name of a town in Kansas or Oklahoma. 'Lovely,' Adelene said, 'is that you?'

The Melody Aces played a Tommy Dorsey medley. Out on the dance-floor couples formed. The cornet player stepped forward and his lips formed the shape of a wife's name before he began to play. Adelene stood up and danced one or two steps, her eyes lost in the complex distances of America.

'Tommy Dorsey,' she said, 'I never heard the like.'

When Adelene went to the toilet Gabriel Hooper looked again at his own face and his wife's face, dazzled by sunlight on zinc barns and rainless seasons of drought and dustbowl politics. He lowered the tip of the cigarette to her face and inhaled the moist, chemical smell of burnt Kodak.

Outside she put her arm through his. They walked out of town until they reached the perimeter fence of the aerodrome.

'What's your wife's name?' she asked.

'Cissy,' he said. It was the sound that sand from the beach made when the wind carried it across concrete.

'Do you think I look like Betty Grable?' she asked. 'They say I'm the dead spit of her.'

She put her back against one of the fence posts and raised her face so that her throat was visible, and he could see, like the faces of an audience, white porcelain insulators on telegraph poles.

'Have you got a rabbit's foot?' she asked. He nodded.

'Where?' He touched the outside of his trouser pocket lightly. Her hand travelled past a handkerchief, a stub of pencil, coins and a brass Zippo to the shreds of tobacco in the pocket lining where there was a soft foot the size of a lost button, and he smiled at the memory of a rabbit surprised in the open on the yellow grass of Kansas or Oklahoma.

A wife's name is the sound that sand makes when the wind carries across concrete. A wife's kiss is the sound of Betty Grable's heart broken with frost in the night. No one knows what a navigator feels when his maps fail him and he looks down and sees all his instruments at zero and the horizon is nowhere in sight.

Nine

By the time the bars had closed and the last few couples
from the Vogue disappeared into the shadows of the towpath where they observed a curfew of promises, Morris had
taken up position in the square. He stood on a lemonade
crate against which he had propped the small worn text
that read: the wages of sin is death.

'The Roman Church is the Whore of Babylon, an abom-
ination in the eyes of God. Friends, the great whore had
me in its clutches. My mortal soul was in grave peril. I
sank into the bottomless pit. I could see no light. Women
and drink, friends. I drank and consorted and knew no
peace within. But, friends, I was saved. As sure as I'm
standing here in front of you, I was washed in the waters
of redemption, and the Lord God abided in my soul, and
I knew everlasting salvation was just around the corner.'

'Would you take a look at that,' a woman in the crowd
said.

'Take a look at what,' the woman standing beside her
said.

'Wait till you see. It's your man.'

'What are you on about? Give us a look.'

'The bastard that near carried the head off you that night. The holy boy.'

'You're having me on.'

'It's no word of a lie.'

'You're right, so you are. I'll tear the shite in two, so I will.'

'Take it easy. Don't be making a show of us.'

'I'll skin him alive.'

Their skins were the colour of naphtha. Their faces were misshapen as if pushed out from the inside by the disappointment of men. Their bodies felt the gravity of standing in damp doorways, the guarantee of the shipyard hooter on paynight, the beatings and complaints of infinite loneliness.

The two women pushed to the front of the crowd. One of them pulled her pleated yellow skirt to the middle of her thigh.

'Come on down here, love,' she shouted, 'I'll give you a rub of the relic.'

Morris stared at the skirt lifted to reveal the forgotten contours of a night spent in an air-raid shelter, and the punishment that was visited on him for that transgression.

The woman turned to face the crowd.

'I'm as holy as that boy. He takes me out one night, chewing the tongue off himself for it so he was. The next day he comes up to me and goes for me.'

She pointed to a small scar beside her eye, half hidden by cyclamen eyeshadow.

'All the height of him and he done that to me. The

blood was tripping me or I would of broke him in two.'

'I never touched her,' Morris said.

'That's not what the Justice said,' the other woman said.

'Go on,' someone shouted from the crowd, 'give her one for Jesus.'

'He did some preaching from the dock of Crumlin Road magistrates' court, so he did,' the first woman said, and laughed.

'I never seen this whore before,' Morris said.

'Mind your tongue,' the woman said, 'or I'll mind it for you.'

'Did you hear what he called us?' the other woman said.

A bottle thrown from the crowd broke against the wall behind Morris. He put his hands up to his face. The two women began to spit at him. His foot slipped from the box and he fell. He could hear laughter.

'For two pins I'd put the skinny bastard over my knee and give him a good skelping.'

'Go for it.'

Morris felt the woman's hands around his waist. He broke away from her and began to run.

Hardy went through the wire of the storage depot with a pair of wire cutters. Ten minutes later they were driving along the perimeter fence with a side of maple-cure bacon, a 40 lb carton of butter, a crate of Dewar's, three packets of Lifebuoy soap, and one stone of coffee beans.

They came across the preacher two miles from the town. Hardy stopped the jeep.

'It's the man of God,' Van der Los said, 'jump in, Reverend.'

Morris was breathing hard, and his coat was hemmed with spit, like green bats hanging from tiny desiccated feet. Without moving from his seat, Van der Los gripped the collar of his coat and pulled him into the back of the jeep.

'Preacher looks shook,' Hardy said. Van der Los handed Morris a bottle and he drank, his neck jerking as he swallowed.

'We hear tell of you, Reverend,' Hardy said, 'you was run out of Belfast.'

'Lock up your daughters when the preacher's around, that's what we hear.'

'It was a mistake.'

'What's he saying?'

It was a mistake. I was tempted by the serpent. I was born loyal to God and to Ulster and caused no affray. She led me astray and removed my wits. I was immersed in the river of salvation. I lifted my fist to her. She gave me a disease.

A contagious infection of the mucous membrane of the genital tract. You observe a yellowish discharge from the affected organ. You experience a burning sensation whilst passing water. Your thought withers.

Hardy parked the jeep behind the Lighthouse café. Morris got out and Van der Los put his large arm over his shoulders. Morris could barely walk under the weight. The man beside him smelt of burnt grass and whiskey. Van der Los pushed him through the door of the bar and ordered drinks with a wave of his free hand.

'We're going to play some cards, preacher,' he said. Hardy sat down in front of them.

'I'm going to tell you a story, preacher,' Van der Los said. 'There's this white pastor with his lady wife and they're walking along these cliffs, outside Capetown, see, and there's two white men leaning over a cliff with a rope and on the end of the rope there's this big kaffir. And the pastor turns to his wife and says to her, "These men are good Christians. See where they strive to save their fellow man from the raging ocean." One of these men, he overhears the pastor. So he turns to the other and says, "This pastor, he knows religion maybe, but he knows fuck-all about shark fishing." What you think of that, eh, preacher?'

'Come in and play some cards,' Hardy said.

The poker game took place in a small storeroom behind the bar. The seats were wooden beer crates and the table was an empty case of Dewar's or Wild Turkey covered with a green baize cloth that Hardy kept in the suitcase under his bed.

'I never played cards with no honest to God Reverend before,' Hardy said.

'Watch him,' Van der Los said, 'damn preacher take your eye out of your socket.'

Outside the café it is night and the seawater gleams on the white pillar of the lighthouse.

'Three-handed poker ain't very satisfactory,' Hardy said, 'but it's better'n nothing. I bet three roasted sinners.'

'Raise you a sulphur pit and chasm ringed with fire,' Van der Los said.

Morris fanned his cards, searching the faces of king, queen and jack as if for some obscure code of damnation, the cipher of temptation fulfilled. They played and drank until first light, Morris winning hand after hand. Hardy threw in the contents of the jeep. Morris won it.

'You're rich, preacher,' Hardy says, 'how many cards?'

'Bet you're after that girl from the canteen that lives in your house.'

'Preacher's got the hots.'

'Two cards for the pastor. Plenty stockings for your girl now, man. Coffee, tea, butter.'

'Sugar for your sugar.'

'Get her little hand inside your breeches.'

'Dealer sticks.'

Hardy talked about the pilot from the Polish Free Army who had joined the poker game in the winter of 1943. The pilot told how he had seen bodies hanging from telegraph poles along a ten-mile stretch of road, the bodies creaking as they turned and the wind singing in the wires and the wires humming with messages of congratulation and accounts of distant war. The Pole drank too much and sang Polish songs in the bar and when they found him in his billet one night toasting a portrait of Churchill with a glass of his own urine they took him away.

Van der Los talked about the townships at night. The smell of cooking fires. Women in doorways who turned sullen at the sight of his white skin but who beckoned by showing wide gums, their teeth pulled painfully with vicegrips so that a man could forget himself between lips removed from the possibility of pain.

As the light changed the room grew as silent as an ill-lit bunker where generals allowed the map of their dreams to unfold on vulnerable sleepers.

Van der Los pushed the last hand away from him and rested his head on his arms. Hardy leaned back in his chair and looked at the scene in front of him as if he had stumbled across signs of skirmish, where the weapons had rusted and the uniforms had become unrecognizable with age. Morris got up and made blindly for the door.

Outside a single plane towing a target took off from the runway and passed low over the roof of the café, the grasses of the mudflats rustling in the backwash. In the distance were the first practice shots from Oerlikons and Bofors guns on the beach. An ambulance pulled up outside the storage depot. No one paid any attention to the figure of the preacher walking along the perimeter road. In the war years there is always a man wheeling a bicycle to work, a lover who has stayed out after curfew finding his way home, a soldier returning from a leave in which he found things as they had always been before and who had discovered in this fact a matter for grief because he had been in the presence of death.

At the storage depot two medical orderlies unpeeled the black sentry from his blood on the concrete and rolled the body on to a stretcher. The stretcher was loaded into the back of an ambulance. The relief sentry who had found the dead man kicked at the half-smoked butt of a Lucky Strike on the ground. In the sentries' billet a military policeman assembled his possessions — clothes, letters, photographs — and began to take inventory of the dead.

Ten

In the evening Mrs Nelligan would give the baby a nip of gin in warm milk to make it sleep and then turn on the wireless. She liked news reports: retreats, offensives, lists of the dead. Sometimes she turned the dial to forgotten radio stations: Moscow, Budapest, Tangiers. The valves hissed like the breath of a million casualties. She listened for the name of her husband among the dead, terrified that the spoken name would bring pain instead of relief.

She was tortured, she reckoned, with the varicose veins. Her ma was took bad with the veins as well and they had taken her leg off when she was only forty. She died roaring for her shoes, thinking that the reason she couldn't walk was that the shoes were hid.

Under the coarse black hair on her ankles and shins the blue veins ran down her legs like tears.

If there was anything worse than the legs it was the ovaries. The ovaries were like stones, the doctor said, and he'd have them out one of these days. First the ovaries and then the legs and the heart would go and she would be in for a landing without an undercarriage in the next world.

Sadie had not been down to eat for three weeks. Mrs Nelligan gave Adelene trays to put outside Sadie's door. Sometimes the trays were taken. Most of the time they sat overnight. Mrs Nelligan could hear the girl moving overhead but then she was quiet for two days and Mrs Nelligan climbed the stairs complaining with a half-bottle of gin in her apron pocket.

The bedroom door wasn't locked. Sadie was sitting on the bed. Mrs Nelligan sat down beside her. The skin around Sadie's eyes was tracked with red as if from staring into the mute westerlies that bring rain from across the Atlantic. Mrs Nelligan poured two glasses of gin and handed one to Sadie.

'It'll do you good,' she said.

'Bud says he can't bear a woman with drink on her breath. Says there's nothing worse than a woman drunk except maybe a woman fighting.'

'The gin is detrimental to heart, lungs and liver. Men's just detrimental, so they are.'

Sadie put the glass to her lips and swallowed.

'Me and Bud's going to have a baby,' she said, 'we're going to open a boarding house in Butte, Montana. I'm saving every penny.'

Mrs Nelligan wondered if the child had lost the bap entirely because she had already guessed what this Bud had done to Sadie, and reckoned that Bud had done the same as Mr Nelligan, who had done a runner as soon as her back was turned.

'When was the last time you seen him?'

'You should see his picture, Mrs Nelligan. He would take the light out of your eye.'

She took a photograph from the drawer beside her bed and gave it to Mrs Nelligan. It was a commercial photographer's dance-hall shot. The couple were smiling up from a table littered with cigarette packets and half-empty glasses, the girl's arms bare, the man leaning back in his chair with a cigarette in his mouth.

Sadie, Mrs Nelligan thought, took a bad picture, and she was no oil painting at the best of times. Bud was different. Sadie was looking at him but he was looking away. Like all men. Called up, transferred or simply blown off course into distant and inaccessible corners of the heart as soon as you looked next or near them. A man'd turn you into a refugee before you knew where you were.

'I have to learn to cook the way the Yanks like it,' Sadie said. From the same drawer she took a sheaf of pages cut from magazines. Recipes for corn bread fritters, pancakes with maple syrup, home fries, she began to turn them over quickly in a way which gave her no time to absorb any of the ingredients or the careful way in which Mrs Nelligan leaned over the bed and touched her stomach.

'When that bastard run out on me,' Mrs Nelligan said, 'I was ready to kill myself. That's no word of a lie.'

But she didn't kill herself. What she did was stand on the tin draining board in the kitchen and jump repeatedly on to the floor, hesitating each time before she jumped, as if the four-foot drop between the sink and the tiles was the long drop into the recollection of stories about knitting needles and wire coathangers, and the old woman with a beard who lived in the houses off the towpath, and the death from haemorrhage.

'Get that gin down your neck,' she said, 'and we'll have another and then I'll pour you a nice hot bath.'

'Tell us he'll come back, Mrs Nelligan,' Sadie said, not believing it herself for the first time, 'he'll come back, won't he?'

'You're only fooling yourself, pet.'

'I love him.'

But Mrs Nelligan has listened to the wireless at night, and in its obscure atmospherics she has heard the voices of the desolate pilots who pack the airways, still handsome in their uniforms of frost.

Eleven

The beach at the end of the runway was deserted at this time of the year. There was a gravel spit and fifty yards of sand. Sometimes a brass shell was washed ashore, green with oxide. On the far side of the spit the bodies of dead birds floated in the grey water until they became waterlogged and sank. At low tide you could see the engine of a P-38 Mustang. The pilot had made one low pass too many over the beach the previous summer to wave down at one of the girls from the canteen. His wingtip touched the water just offshore and the plane cartwheeled for as long as it takes to travel the distance between an oily patch in the shallow water and the frozen smile on the face of a girl in a yellow bathing suit.

Hooper drove a borrowed jeep over the dunes towards the beach. Adelene sat beside him wearing a headscarf. He stopped the jeep at the edge of the sand and Adelene got out.

'God, I love the beach, so I do,' she said, 'bring us out the camera there.'

She kicked off her shoes and ran as far as the water.

'Don't look,' she said, as she began to roll her stockings down her legs.

Slipping them over her calves, she stepped out of them

so that they remained for a moment in the shape of a man kneeling, then collapsed on to the sand.

'You looked,' she said, then ran into the sea. Hooper lifted the camera to his eyes to photograph her, eyes wide as the cold water stung her bare legs. Hooper had already developed photographs of Adelene and stuck them to the door of his locker beside Betty Grable. Adelene standing against the perimeter fence. Adelene outside the Vogue. Adelene on the big dipper the day they drove up the coast, clutching the handrail with one hand and trying with the other to hold down the skirt of her print frock which had blown up to reveal a palm-sized flash of white, like an evacuee face glimpsed from the moving window of a refugee train. He kept the paper envelopes the photographs came in on the locker beside his bed and would wake at night to the smell of developing fluid and look over to where the envelopes mounted like consolations assembled for the future.

Later Hooper parked the jeep on the dunes and Adelene lay with her head across his knees. He talked about the place he came from. The Saturday nights, the bad harvests, the clear sky when you lay awake at night. She stroked the material of his trousers and looked up at his face above the polished buttons of his uniform. It seemed to her as if he was talking out of some distant interior world of chrome, dirt roads and stars.

He grew silent when she started to talk about herself. She had caught him watching her as if she had disembarked into his war years with the opening credits already rolling and her face and figure undisturbed by small histories.

She told him about the draper's shop on the Antrim Road in the city. Films at the Curzon. The night the Germans bombed the waterworks, when everyone knew it was the Jewmen who lived on the Antrim Road they were after. How they never found hide nor hair of her father afterwards, because he refused to go to the shelter when the air-raid siren went off, but continued cutting cloth for officers' uniforms at the counter.

She did not mention how she dreamed of her father standing at the counter while the air quivered with the sound of heavy bombers, his fingers moving on the brass ruler inset on the counter as if to measure the fabric of a sudden, lethal uncertainty.

She spent the next night in fields outside the city with the smell of burning oil from the shipyard in her nostrils. She came to Cranfield on the train the following night, passing through empty fields and blacked-out towns and stations with long-deserted platforms. Exhausted soldiers slept on their kitbags in the corridor of the train while she plucked her eyebrows in the toilet cubicle and cried. The train was carrying her behind hostile lines into a territory where she would survive like Betty Grable without memory.

Hooper watched her with the expression of a man watching something mournful falling from a plains sky.

*

Later she sat at her dressing table scratching an insect bite on her thigh. Hooper crossed the room, the cold linoleum creaking under his feet, and slipped his hand over her shoulder, watching her eyes widen in the mirror, his hand coming to rest over Betty Grable's negligent heart.

Later, when she slept, Hooper got up and dressed. She turned in her sleep and the sheets crackled like parachute silk drifting over ploughed field or open sea. He listened to her breathing. It was the sound of Betty Grable's bare feet stalking you across boarding-house floors and other empty places in your mind. He closed the door quietly and went down the stairs. When he got to the hallway the parlour door opened and Mrs Nelligan fell against him. She had lipstick on her teeth and there was a smell of gin.

'Were you ever', she moaned, 'crossed in love?'

Twelve

At the beginning of February storm-force winds crossed the country. The wireless spoke of convoys dispersed and ships running blind. All flights were grounded for a week.

All that week Sadie walked into the town to look for Bud. When it rained she stood in the foyer of the Vogue looking out through the plate glass window, which shivered as if it was about to blow away as a bright tile in the wind. But the truck from the aerodrome did not come during the week, and there was no one else in the foyer except the girl in the box office. Sadie smoked cigarette after cigarette. The girl in the box office licked her thumb to turn another page of the magazine she held under the counter. These are the disappointed hours when Betty Grable leans out from the coming attractions case offering the counterfeits of home: distant lights, the smell of deserted terminals, the sound of rain.

The balcony doors opened and the manager came down the stairs carrying a torch. He unlocked the door of the box office and went in. He put the torch on the counter and took out the tin box containing the takings.

'Quiet as a grave in there,' he said, leaning back against

the counter and putting his hands in his pockets.

'Are you for the Vogue tonight?' he asked.

'I'm for my bed. The feet's cut off me standing here.'

'Arse rid off you, more like.'

'Kiss my ass,' she said.

'Kiss my ass,' he repeated, 'you never learned that Yank talk by going home at night.'

'Smart.'

'I use the head. Not like your woman over there.' He nodded in the direction of Sadie.

'Deserves all she gets,' the girl said, examining her nails.

'I'd say she got more than she bargained for, by the look of her.'

'You'd have to be as thick as bottled pigshite to believe anything them Yanks tell you.'

'I suppose you're not?'

'I use the head.'

Outside a truck swerved as the wind caught it and lurched over a kerb. Sadie crossed to the window and watched for men dismounting.

'A bad case,' the manager said.

'Men's all the same.'

Sadie watched two men unloading crates from the lorry. When they had finished they got back into the cab. Sadie ground her cigarette out on the floor and walked to the door. Outside the wind blew her coat against her so that the pregnancy was visible.

'Coming attractions,' the girl in the box office said

bitterly, watching Sadie move off into the wind as the truck passed her, its hooded headlights disappearing into a landscape of the discarded.

Hardy and Van der Los were at the bar of the Lighthouse.

'You shouldn't of hit him so hard,' Hardy said.

'Don't worry,' Van der Los said, 'no one's going to find out.'

'There was this drover once, killed a girl,' Hardy said. But he didn't finish it. He remembered how they had queued for hours outside the courthouse to be in for the kill: the trial, the verdict, the turning of the drover's legs to water and the two cops who carried him out of the dock when all you could hear in the courtroom was his mother crying into a handkerchief and saying he done it for love.

'You shouldn't of done it,' Hardy repeated.

'You see them looking at our girls?' Van der Los asked. His eyes were bloodshot. He brought his face close to Hardy's, his lips drawn tight over his teeth and his breath feral.

'Birds, blacks, man. This damn war kill us all. I hear you speak a word about this I kill you too.'

The black guard hadn't heard them come up behind him. Van der Los had swung the heavy bolt cutters and hit him behind the ear. They had loaded the jeep and then while Hardy waited in the driver's seat Van der Los had gone back.

'I think you're crazy,' Hardy whispered. Van der Los grinned and put his rank, powerful arm over Hardy's shoulders. Hardy pulled away and made for the door. Behind him he could hear Van der Los laughing.

Hooper got the letter the next morning as he was preparing a class. The paper of the envelope was thin, like the paper in a hatbox. There was a Chicago postmark. He turned it over in hands that trembled like the stained glass of cathedrals in Rheims or Coventry. He leaned his head against the barrel of the telescope. Yellow foam from the sea blew across the apron, sticking to hangar walls and exposed aircraft cowlings. The window creaked in its putty.

There were weather maps spread out on the bed behind him. He had marked windspeeds and pressure in red pen across the charts with projections for the next twenty-four hours added in green pen, and anticyclones and cold fronts in blue.

He ripped the letter open with his fingernail, knowing that his wife had decided to take her chances.

Dear Gabriel

I have left our house and the things of our life together. I writ to you before for you to get your skates on and come back but I tore it up. I sold the stock and the money's yours except for what I took with me. There were times I wished I never set eyes on you but I don't feel that

now. In case you think, there isn't anybody else. I got a
job here and a place so I'm alright but I never thought it
would be so cold. I don't know what to say. You never
noticed I was there before. I have the land let for a year to
Joe Parry, which paid some of the bank but I don't know
what you'll do next year. I had to buy a new coat when I
got here. This is the first new thing I had in years. I hope
things are fine for you.

    Love

      Cissy

P.S. I put no address on the letter so don't try to find me.
It wouldn't make no difference. That's the truth.

It was as if he could hear her voice telling him of days
spent alone in the kitchen or the yard, or down in the barn
among the meal sacks, the patent horse medicines, the
knotholes and the dust settling on the places he never
touched.

A wife's name is the sound that sand makes when the
wind carries it across concrete. A wife's kiss is the sound
of Betty Grable's heart broken with frost in the night.
Gabriel Hooper walked to the window to look for America,
but it was lost in an advancing frontal system, weather in
which men find themselves mapless and bereft.

Thirteen

Bombers from the squadron joined the raid on Dresden. Hardy followed the bombers in through the sparse anti-aircraft fire, returning with 8 × 10 photographs bleached white with phosphorus. He overflew the city again the next day for low-level shots of railway marshalling yards, factories and buildings collapsed inwards on streets where small figures walked, following the obliterated pavements as if they were the impaired diagrams of home.

At night Morris went to the square. His eyes were bloodshot and there was lint in his uncombed hair. No one stopped to listen. He tried to recall the speakers he had heard when he was young, Carson, or Roaring Hanna. But their voice gets louder with the years and your own voice fades to a point under the stars and then is still.

He gave up and stayed in his room. When he shut his eyes he could see Adelene walking arm in arm with a man in uniform. He could see himself as a child standing in the doorway of his mother's bedroom. A man's body flickers like a light between a woman's thighs and then goes out.

He could see himself severed from the living God and susceptible to vice.

Adelene got up and went to the bathroom. The door was closed. She went away and came back and then knocked.

'God, Sadie,' she said, 'are you not out of that bath yet?' She tried the door and it opened. Sadie was lying on her back in the enamel tub. There was a drip from the old chrome-plated tap which had the brass showing through like a taste. There was an empty gin bottle on the washstand and the water in the bath was pink. Afterwards Mrs Nelligan said she couldn't get over it. Lying there all night with the water getting cold around her like Odessa or one of them places.

Adelene sat beside her in the ambulance, looking down at her grey, peaceful face on the stretcher like one of those women you saw on newsreels pushing prams out of rubble, collecting picture frames, broken gramophones, the roof over your head, the ground beneath your feet. Men is detrimental, Mrs Nelligan said, and that's the God's honest truth.

When Hooper got to the house Mrs Nelligan was sitting on the sofa in the front parlour.

'Where's Adelene?'

'You'll have a drink, Sergeant.'

'Is she in her room?'

'Sit down, Sergeant, and give us a while of your chat.'

'Maybe later, Mrs Nelligan.'

'Get yourself a glass from the press, there's a pet. That Mr Roosevelt doesn't look well in himself.'

Hooper went up the stairs. He hesitated outside her door, then knocked. She opened it wearing a dressing gown. Her hair was held back with a band and there was cold cream on her face. She kissed him and went back to the dressing table, sitting with her back to him as she told him what happened to Sadie. Her face was indistinct in the mirror, and her voice was barely audible. It was the way in which Hooper had seen Polish airmen discuss their own country, threading their way among the rumours of massacre and unreported execution. Then they'd fall silent, as if they had found themselves in a forest clearing where the freshly dug earth had hardened, the temperature degrees below zero, with the sharing of pain palpable in the air between them like the smell of cordite.

She turned to face him.

'If you've something to say, Gabriel, you'd better say it.' She watched him carefully. He could not remember her using his first name before and it came like a reprisal.

'I put in for a transfer back to the States.'

She turned back to the mirror so that he couldn't see her face.

'The war's near over, isn't it?' she said. Her voice was uncertain, as if the war and this room had already become part of memory, a haunted look in the eyes. They could hear sparse, residual firing from the beach. She looked out of the window as if she would see herself walking through the war years wearing breathless high heels and stockings that fit her legs like memory itself.

'Couple of months,' he said. He was still standing in the doorway with his hands in his pockets.

'What are you going to do?' he asked.

'Don't know. Back to the city, maybe. You?'

'Couldn't tell you. She left.'

Adelene went on cleaning her face. Wiping the hollows around her eyes, the cotton wool dragging her eyelids down, kissing lipstick on to a tissue. Hooper walked across the room. He picked up a tissue and looked at it, seeing the fine mesh of lines imprinted on it. He lifted his hand to put it on her shoulder, then dropped it again, as if she had wandered off the grid, and he had failed to locate her.

'You know what I done before the war?' she asked. He shook his head.

'I worked in the shirt factory. I always wanted to work in the picture-house. Go around with a torch, you know. I suppose one job's the same as another.'

She wanted to shine the torch through the blue smoke that lay like a net over the stalls and the balcony, picking out the faces of the lovers and the unloved and the way they looked at the screen, as if there was something up there that had something to do with them, but that they couldn't put their finger on.

'The shirt factory got blew up the first night of the blitz,' she said.

'Take us to the dance tomorrow night,' she said. Take me to the dance. Tell me the names of the stars. Walk out along the perimeter fence and look at me like there's something but you just can't put your finger on it.

'I'll pick you up,' he said. He went out and closed the door behind him.

When Hooper got back to the aerodrome Hardy was lying across his bed, drunk. He turned over when Hooper came in.

'Didn't mean to wake you,' Hooper said.

'Wasn't really sleeping anyhow. Hear about that negro got himself killed?'

'Cut bad, I hear.'

'Shouldn't have gone messing with our girls. I can't abide that.'

Hooper sat down on his own bed. The torn airmail envelope was on the bedside locker along with the developed films.

'Are you going to stay in the Air Force after the war, Hooper?'

'I couldn't tell you.'

'They say you're the best navigator on the base. Do a three-point fix in less than a minute. Navigate your way around a woman anyhow.' Hardy nodded at the photographs of Adelene on the locker door. 'You got a wife, Hooper? I ain't. Never had luck with women. No luck. Had a girl here. Never had no luck with her neither. Like them teenage whores they had at the training camp. Roundheels. One of them comes up to me one night, I'm drinking, you know? Says I've to help her with this vital war work. So we goes outside and round the back of the bar. I'm there doing this vital war work on her and she's just looking up at me. Like I was something she'd just pulled over her to keep out the cold and the sound of them barges on the river and this grass on the lot all oily and frozen stiff and her making no noise at all.'

Hardy's voice faded. Hooper turned to look at him.

'You OK?'

'Nigger didn't have no business being there, Hooper,' Hardy said, 'I never meant to do nothing, but he didn't have no business there.'

Hardy's breath was coming fast.

'You're sweating like a pig,' Hooper said.

'They'll take me away,' Hardy said, 'and I never even been in love. You been in love, Hooper?'

But Hooper knows that love's a widow in the spring of 1945. There's a straight black line running from the heel of her black court shoes to your heart. You'll hear her moan through lips discoloured by grief. You'll dream of her, whose name is Sorrow.

Fourteen

In the morning Hooper ran a steel comb through his hair and walked to the window. He could see the white alkaloid flare of a cutting torch behind the hangars and a pennant of blue filings from a circular saw. On the perimeter of the aerodrome war was dismantling itself into the names of cities, the possessions of the dead, thoughts of home. In the distance rain scratched the tin roofs of Nissen huts and hangars. Driven inland by an advancing frontal system, seagulls squatted at the wet black edge of the runway.

The preacher's suitcase held a pair of socks, a bundle of pamphlets tied with string and a razor with beads of rust on the blade. It was lined with an old *Belfast Telegraph*. The front page carried a photograph of gutted buildings, doors and windows opening on to empty parlours and strips of wallpaper hanging from gable walls and floorless bedrooms furnished with loss.

Morris took the razor from the suitcase and soaped his face at the washstand in the corner of the room. His mind blew like leaves through backstreet histories. He had seen

Hooper and Adelene at the gate put their arms around each other and walk slowly away from him towards the town. He prepared to follow them. If he had to he would go on his knees to her and ask forgiveness for the emptiness that occupied his heart.

Thou art all fair, my love; there is no spot on thee.

The Vogue was half empty. The squadrons based at the aerodrome were gradually being transferred to the Pacific. Adelene left Hooper to go to the ladies. He went to the balcony to wait for her. The only women on the dance-floor below were the parachute packers from the aerodrome. The parachute packers worked with a jar of hand cream beside them, and their nails were cut to the quick to avoid snagging the silk. They sat along the wall opposite the band with their spotless hands folded in their laps as if they held there the knowledge of falling. Hooper's eyes searched their faces as if he would see his wife as she had been, dolled up to the nines and speechless with love.

Adelene looked up at him as she crossed the dance-floor. She had seen enough partings. Girls standing at the perimeter fence drenched by the backwash of a DC-9 transporter, the light of its exhausts receding towards the runway until only the wet flap of a USAF flag like the loose end of film turning in the projector was left. In her room she kept a drawerful of mementoes of her own partings: photographs, lighters, nickels and dimes, censored letters that suddenly stopped coming and letters she had written herself, returned without explanation. She would open these and read her own handwriting as if the letter was the history of someone else's life.

Morris stood in front of the band. He had cut himself shaving, and there was a piece of tissue hanging from his lip that flickered with his breathing. He looked for Adelene among the threads of cornet spit, the smell of Lifebuoy and cigarettes and floor polish and the conversation of men for whom this would be the last dance because they would be leaving soon to fly missions out of Pearl Harbor, Guadalcanal, the Philippines. Going out on a khaki wind to skid, in the last days of war, from carrier decks sticky with rubber and dried salt and spilled aviation fuel.

Adelene and Hooper moved out on to the dance-floor. When they danced Hooper's hand in the small of her back would guide her, as if on some flight path mapped out with precision, so that she felt when she met him that he would steer her indefinitely along the abandoned routes between desire and regret. But this time she felt that he barely held her. She looked up at the band. The lead singer wore a grey suit and looked like a knife. That's what men are, she thought, them met the preacher's eyes when she looked down from the band. She saw the open razor in his hand.

A week before he got married Hooper had bought a suit for $25. Cissy had turned the collar and cuffs and sewn leather patches on to the elbows when it became clear that they could not afford another one. When he got to the induction camp he had taken his call-up papers and his rabbit's foot out of the trouser pocket, then wrapped it in brown paper and handed it in. Earlier that day he had wondered if it would still be there when he got back and that wearing it he would be able to remember the names of all the railway stations on the way home and what people did in Chicago when the snow was gone.

Hardy saw what was happening from the balcony and leapt the balustrade, crashing into couples dancing inches apart to 'Melancholy Baby'. But by the time he got to the front of the stage Hooper was already on the ground with a white-lipped cut in his throat and the butt of his cigarette burning a black fingernail in the waxed boards beside his head. The preacher and Adelene stood on either side of him. Morris looked at the razor in his hand as if it was his own tongue, snatched from the eternal fire.

It was as if the pilot had stepped into his $25 suit and walked away from them towards the sound of a voice that he knew. Before the stretcher bearers took him away, Adelene slipped her hand into his trouser pocket and removed the rabbit's foot.

By the time an ambulance had arrived the lips of the wound had turned black and curled upwards in a smile of impenetrable memory.

Hardy pinned Morris against the edge of the stage, gripping the loose, yellow flesh of his throat in one fist, as if the preacher's body was a suitcase packed for a long journey and his throat was the handle. Morris's small eyes followed Adelene's every move even when the Military Police removed him, his feet dragging on the ground. He was unable to speak or to appeal to her to turn in his direction, just one glance that would be his redemption.

Outside Adelene watched the ambulance drive in the direction of the aerodrome. Across the street she could see Betty Grable in the coming attractions case. The glass was fly-specked and the edges of the paper were beginning to curl but her hands were outstretched, palm upwards, as if to weigh the sorrow that a war deposits in the hearts of women.

Back in her bedroom she opened the drawer where she kept her mementoes with numb fingers and took the rabbit's foot out of her pocket. She lifted it to her mouth. It was light in her palm like a corn husk. She touched it to her lips and tried to think of a rabbit cleaning its ears beside a burrow in Kansas or Oklahoma. She set it down. Lying on top of the other photographs in the drawer was one they'd had taken at the amusements in Warrenpoint. The pocket of a dead pilot is often found to contain a rabbit's foot or photobooth snapshot from a port entrance or railway station or other point of departure. She felt that if she got up and looked in the mirror, the face she would see would be barely recognizable as the one in the photograph. She'd see the face of someone who was a survivor of

uncertain wars fought in velvet balcony seats and across the
unnavigable terrain of men sick for home.

One night she had come in late. Sadie was sitting on
her bed waiting for her. When she took off her blouse Sadie
laughed because the perimeter fence had imprinted itself
on her back.

She put the photograph back in the drawer and then
took a case from under the bed and began to pack. It
was over. There were no more silk stockings or American
chocolate. No more coming home with the first daylight
sortie passing overhead and the reedheads of the mudflats
showing white undersides and the sun picking out rivets
on the bottom of each aluminium fuselage. No more men
falling helpless. No more canteen counter with pilots looking from her face to the clock as if to set out points of
reference they would carry in their heads into hostile airspace. No more Dear John.

There was a light tap on Adelene's door. Mrs Nelligan was
standing outside. She put her hand on the girl's arm.

'There's someone downstairs wants a word with you,
pet.'

Hardy was sitting on the sofa in the parlour. He got to
his feet when Adelene came in. He had his forage cap in
his hands.

'I brought something,' he said, nodding at the pile of
photographs on the table, as if he had carried them from
overseas like a dying man's last words.

'They're flying him home tomorrow,' he said, 'full military honours and all.' Adelene sat down beside him. Mrs Nelligan went to the glass-fronted cabinet for glasses. Hardy's face was distant and strained, intent on horizons. Mrs Nelligan poured gin. The baby shifted in its pram.

'They got Van de Los,' Hardy said softly, 'him 'n the preacher both. They can sing hymns to each other in the glasshouse. Van der Los just couldn't help boasting, I suppose. War's over for me now anyhow. Did you ever wish you hadn't done things?'

'What'd you do?' Mrs Nelligan asked, leaning forward in her chair because she'd seen his face before.

'Weren't me,' he said, 'all I done was a bit of robbing. Was Van der Los killed the nigger.'

'I seen you before,' Mrs Nelligan said suddenly, as if she'd already fingerprinted, tried and condemned him for some unknown crime of the heart.

'I don't reckon so,' Hardy replied, seeing Van der Los sitting in the back of a military police jeep looking nervous as a plains animal at noon. He'd spill the beans all right.

Hardy stood up to go, brushing the front of his uniform.

'He was a good man,' he said slowly, 'could do a three-point fix quicker'n any man I ever seen. I reckoned seeing as you wouldn't get no official visit or anything I'd come down and bring you something of his.'

'I got something,' Adelene said, 'you can hold on to them photos. Wouldn't do me any good anyhow.'

'Didn't mean no harm, now.'

'I know.'

Hardy lifted the photographs and tipped the peak of his cap. Adelene followed him silently to the hall door and closed it behind him. Mrs Nelligan heard her feet on the stairs and remembered where she had seen Hardy before. It was the moustache that done it and the way he sat, with his long legs stretched out in front of him – the way he was in the photograph Sadie showed her. Men is detrimental. Mrs Nelligan poured herself a gin and promised to be silent for ever. If Sadie believed he was dead and gone that was all the better. She lifted the glass to toast herself and others, crossed in love.

Fifteen

Adelene and Sadie stood on the northbound platform. There was no one else waiting for the Belfast train. There was a smell of soot and paraffin from the leaking stove in the waiting room behind them. Adelene put down her suitcase and sat on a wooden bench. Sadie stayed on her feet, looking towards the horizon where the runway lights crossed the skyline like the lights of a thousand Dodge sedans travelling west.

'I hope he's hung,' Sadie said.

'Who?'

'Morris. What did he go and do that for?'

'Couldn't tell you.'

'I hope he's hung, anyhow.'

Adelene used her finger to trace the names that had been scratched on the paint, some with dates like map references. Sadie sat down beside her, placing her fat hand over Adelene's. After the haemorrhage Sadie had not lost weight, but there was a darkness on her fair skin like smudged newsprint, the unreadable headlines of remote conflict.

Adelene tried to make her mind dwell on her destination.

The houses under the shipyard gantries, factory hooters, bakeries and the dawn over its industrial rivers. But her mind crossed it like the shadow of a plane cast on the ground at daylight. A shadow made up of the smoke of burning cities and the movement of populations.

A man crossed the footbridge and came down the iron stairs with an unlit cigarette in his lips. He wore an uncreased uniform with fresh sergeant's stripes on the sleeve. He hesitated, then walked up the platform towards them, stopping in front of Adelene.

'Hey Betty,' he said, 'give us a light for a cigarette.'

He bent to take the light from her hands. As he straightened he looked into her face and was held by a long bereaved stare. After a few seconds he backed away, apologizing.

You'll go back to some barracks, Adelene thought, and write letters to your young wife, and lie on your bed at night staring at Betty Grable and dreaming of slipping the straps from her uncomplaining shoulders and folding the material of her swimming suit to her waist. There was the sound of a train approaching. The two women stood up and picked up their suitcases.

If you look back from the window of a moving train you will see a man in uniform with an unlit cigarette between his lips watching your departure. If you turn away then look again he will be gone. If you see a poster of Betty Grable in some deserted station, her breasts will be as smooth as the cone of a navigator's unreliable pencil. If you pull down the top of her swimming costume her breasts accuse and her navel is a spotlight scanning the skyline of Europe for love in history, finding you then losing you between gaps in the clouds.